Sophie

Sophie

Tal Tsfany

Illustrated by Ron Tsfany

ISBN: 197784555X
ISBN-13: 9781977845559
Library of Congress Control Number: 2017917558
CreateSpace Independent Publishing Platform
North Charleston, South Carolina

To my "Tsfunnies"—Hagita, Ronchubonchu, Shirilula, and Yaelibeli.
And to the real Sophie and Leo.

CONTENTS

PREFACE

Several years ago, I read a book that changed my life.

The protagonist's uncompromising principles and unwavering character made a lasting impression on me. The profound philosophical ideas underlying the story evoked a burning desire in me to express them in a way my kids could understand. I started writing short stories and read them to my youngest daughter Yael. After finishing a story, we'd have meaningful discussions about the morals of those stories.

The idea of parents and kids discussing philosophical concepts motivated me to create my own story and heroine.

So here is *Sophie*—I hope she stirs some poignant conversations and helps you understand how to live life a little better.

I want to thank my friends and family who contributed to the process of writing and publishing *Sophie*, especially: Hagit, Ron, Shiri and Yaeli, who supported me in every step of the way. To Marianna Brashear, Nathalie Apteker, Alon Zaibert, Lior Weinstein, and Hadar Mendelevitz-Bengal for their valuable advice and feedback.

And to all who believed in Sophie before she came out into the world: Peter and Christina, Anir, Emilie, Jonathan, Craig, Darcy, Ima, Aba, Dafna, Rinat M., Alon, Michal, Uzi, Einat, Guy, Sagive, Laura, Vic, Richard, Michael S., Ashish, Lars, Josh, Andrew, Piotr M., Yoav and Boaz L., Dror, Lizi, Lauren, Joel M., Michael C., Eitan, Hilit, Marsha, Erez, Roi, Stephen, Eyal, Ron, Steven R. Steven B., Barak, Seavan, Piotr N., Jeri, Rinat G., Mark, Adam, Nava, Yoni, Tsipi, Leon, Boaz M., Shea, Shely, Alexis, Lee, Shiri, Gil, Bart, Noam, Mahesh, Joelle, Brandi, Elise, Yariv, Kison, Selena, Yael, Mikita, Pooja, Lior, Joel G., Matt, Uri, Eli, Michael F., Gili, Paul, Ken, Carlos, Kumar, Eleanor, Esther, Evan, Lauren C., Lulu, Aviv, Itai, and Amit.

CHAPTER 1

THE GIRL WITH THE BOOK

Here I am again.

In this small hometown of mine, in the middle of nowhere. Standing next to this big old oak tree, as I have done so many times before. And that same feeling of anticipation crawls up my chest again.

I missed it so much. I've missed her so much.

I can clearly remember the first time I met her.

It was a hot afternoon during summer break, a day before I turned thirteen. I was riding my bike, pedaling fast, trying to catch up with my friends, who had already left the park on their way to the open fields.

As I came closer to the edge of the trail that cut through the park's big lawn, I slowed down. A dark-haired girl in a worn-out striped shirt sat beneath this very same oak.

Something about that quiet, unfamiliar face made me stop. Maybe it was the way she sat there, hugging her knees to her chest, staring at the open book that lay on the grass in front of her. She was so focused on that book, as if the world around her didn't exist.

I stopped, knowing there was no way I would catch up with my bike buddies. I leaned my bicycle against the tree and walked up to her until I was quite close. She didn't notice me. I walked a little closer and... nothing. She was in a bubble, separated from the outside world by that book.

A thought crossed my mind—what if she *had* noticed me but chose to ignore me? Maybe she was hoping I would just go away and leave her alone to read quietly.

For a brief moment, I thought of turning back to my bike, but a second later, I heard myself ask, "What are you reading?"

The girl looked up, squinting and shading her eyes from the afternoon sun.

"Do you mind moving a little so I can see who I'm talking to?" she asked with a touch of a foreign accent I had never heard before.

"I'm Leo, Leo Weckl," I answered, moving to my left so my shadow would fall on her face. "I live on the other side of the park. Are you from around here? I haven't seen you here before."

"You couldn't have. We moved here only a couple of days ago," the girl said, lowering her head toward her book. "And to answer your first question"—she paused briefly— "it's a biography."

"Oh...OK." I hesitated. It took me a second to recall that I had started with asking her a question about the book.

"Where are you from?" I kept going, wondering about her accent.

The girl looked up at me and froze for several seconds. Then she lowered her head again and said, almost whispering, "Originally from the Middle East, but I'm here now, right?"

I wasn't sure what to say next. I stood there for a couple of awkward seconds, putting my hands in my jeans pockets and trying to recall what had made me decide to stop and talk to that girl. I didn't know what it was, but I still felt it.

Ready to admit defeat, I was about to turn back to my bike. Right then, the girl swiftly picked up her book from the grass, closed it, and put it under her arm. She stood up and looked straight at me with deep jet-black eyes. Her look was so direct and intense that I felt the need to look away.

But I didn't.

I looked straight back at her as if to pay her back for making me feel uncomfortable. We stood there for a brief moment, looking at each other as though we were in a staring contest.

It was strange to look that way at someone I'd just met; it felt different. That girl was clearly not from around here. No one that I knew would look at you this way. I started fiddling with a loose thread inside my jeans pocket, and tried my best not to take my eyes off of her.

She finally spoke up. "So, if you live on the other side of the park, that means we're neighbors. I live in that brown house." She pointed at the old house on the other side of the street.

The brown house had belonged to an elderly couple who'd left to go to a nursing home just several months before. I'd heard that when developers built our neighborhood, the old couple didn't want to move, so the company had kept that house at the entrance of it and fitted the park and new homes around them.

We called them "the Draculas" because no one ever saw them leave their house during the day, and whenever a football or soccer ball fell into their high-fenced garden, we would find it in the park, sliced open the next day.

Kids in our neighborhood made up creepy stories about that couple and their haunted house.

The brown house had stood empty for months, and it looked dirty and dusty. Some roof shingles were missing, and the fence surrounding the house was falling apart.

"Oh, so the moving truck that left all that stuff on the sidewalk next to that house—that was yours!" I recalled the noisy truck my mother and her friends had been complaining about a couple of days earlier. It had been the talk of the day, as a couple of mattresses and piles of boxes had been scattered all over the sidewalk for several hours.

"It looked like a real mess," I said. A moment later, I realized my words might have hurt her feelings. I cleared my throat, sounding louder than I had intended for it to be, making that moment even more awkward.

The girl looked at me, and instead of being offended, she grinned.

"The movers decided they wanted more money than what we had originally agreed on. I wouldn't budge, so they threw our things on the sidewalk and left. My mother and I had to carry everything inside, but it wasn't so bad after all—when we got everything inside, she was so tired that I got to decide how to organize things around the house."

The girl said some of the words in a strange accent, but her voice was clear and confident.

"Why didn't you pay them? Did they ask for too much?" I thought that if it had been *my* stuff out there on the sidewalk for everyone to see, I probably would have paid the movers just to avoid the embarrassment.

"We just couldn't afford it. We don't have much money. This house was actually cheaper to rent than a small apartment somewhere else," she replied without hesitation.

"Oh...I see." I was a little surprised by her direct answer.

The girl noticed I was trying to catch the title of the book she was holding under her arm.

"It's a book about Thomas Jefferson," she offered. "I got it from the library. I love having a library so close by." She pointed toward the neighborhood's entrance, which led to the library on the hill on the other side of the road.

"Do you like to read?" she asked. There was a hint of excitement in her voice, and for the first time since we'd started talking, I felt she was interested in the conversation. She had this half smile on her face, and her eyes were wide open. I felt more relaxed and smiled back at her, took my hands out of my pockets, and crossed my arms over my chest.

"I'm more into drawing," I admitted, "but I love a good story."

"What do you draw?" The girl sounded impressed.

"All kinds of things, but mainly fantasy characters." I looked down. I had never shared my drawings with anyone. They were my little secret hidden in the back of my closet.

"What kind of characters?" She leaned forward, trying to make me look up again.

"All kinds—mainly superheroes and Japanese manga characters that I come up with." I shrugged and raised my head to look at her again. It felt weird to be sharing something like this with a stranger I'd met five minutes ago.

"I love manga!" Her eyes opened excitedly. "Those faces with the huge, sparkling eyes and big mouths…"

"Yes. Wow…most people have never even heard of it."

"Will you show me one of your characters?" The girl rocked forward and lifted herself up on her toes for a brief moment.

I'd been afraid she'd ask that but found myself immediately considering which one I should show her. "I guess," I said, "but don't expect too much— I'm not that good. There are some amazing artists out there who—"

"You mean to say that you're not that good...*yet*," she said, interrupting me.

"Maybe...but still, don't get your expectations too high."

"Are you saying that because yours are?"

"What do you mean?" I tilted my head a little.

"Your expectations—are they too high?" she repeated.

"I don't know," I blurted, but then it hit me that she was probably right. I gazed at her, thinking about how every time I finished a drawing, I felt frustrated rather than satisfied—because I was comparing my work with the comic books I was reading. Maybe that was also the reason I wouldn't show my characters to anyone. Perhaps a thirteen-year-old boy *shouldn't* expect to be as good as a grown-up artist. That suddenly made so much sense to me.

How can she know all that about me already? I thought, squinting at her.

The sun was low in the sky and washed the girl's face with a golden-orange color. The sound of kids yelling and laughing in the nearby playground rolled around the park.

"Well, I need to get going," she said. She picked up a plastic bag containing one red apple from the ground. "It's getting late, and I have many things to do. I guess I'll see you soon." She smiled, her hands crossed around Jefferson.

I went back to my bicycle as the girl started walking back toward the brown house. I stood by the thick oak's trunk, watching her walk away.

"Hey, you didn't tell me your name," I yelled.

The girl stopped in her tracks. It seemed like my words had surprised her. After a quick second of standing still with her back toward me, she turned around quickly. Then, instead of just yelling her name back, she started pacing toward me. I walked a couple of steps in her direction.

She got closer and extended her hand to shake mine. "That was rude of me. I'm Sophia—Sophia Anwar, but you can call me Sophie. The *a* in the end just takes up too much time. That is assuming you are going to call my name often, which I hope you will." She smiled, and I smiled back.

"I'm Leo Weckl," I said just as we released our handshake.

"I know. You already told me."

Sophie turned around and started walking toward her house. I watched her and noticed she looked taller than she was. Her back was erect, as if an invisible thread was pulling her upward, making her taller and lighter. She held her head high as if hovering an inch above the ground, gently and effortlessly.

I stood there, holding the handlebars of my bike, my eyes fixed on Sophie as she walked back to the old brown house.

"There's something strange about that girl," I said to myself as I turned around to ride back home.

What I really meant was that I thought she was special.

CHAPTER 2

ORTHEA

A week or so later, I rode my bike through the park with three other friends. As we got closer to the playground area, I recognized the same dark hair falling around Sophie's face as she leaned forward.

She was sitting on one of the park's wooden benches, one leg crossed over the other, reading a book. This time, she looked up and smiled at me.

"I'll catch you guys later." I nodded to my friends, who stopped and looked back as I slowed next to Sophie. I could hear them giggling and whispering to one another as they rode away.

"Hey," I said as I got off my bike.

"Hey to you too." Sophie sat up straight, the book lying open on her lap.

"Reading again?" I asked.

Sophie nodded, smiling. "Whenever I can." As I got closer to her, I suddenly felt a rush of blood washing my cheeks, making my face warm and tingly. I hated when that happened.

"Do you want to go get some ice cream?" I suggested, trying not to think about how red my face must have looked.

"Let's do that." Sophie hopped off the bench.

"Hop on the back rack. It'll be faster," I said, getting back on my bike. Sophie got on behind me without hesitation, and we rode to the nearby strip mall to get ice cream.

When we got to the ice cream parlor, Sophie said she wasn't getting any.

"I'm buying, Sophie," I said, guessing she might not have the money for it, but Sophie insisted she was OK. I took my usual plain chocolate scoop in a waffle cone, and we started walking back home, Sophie pushing my bike by the handles.

On our way back, we stopped next to a toy shop that had a beautiful orange skateboard on display in the front window.

"It's the wide-wheel Rocket model," I said. "It's made by an Australian company, and it's considered one of the best in the world."

Sophie leaned forward, her nose nearly touching the window as she looked carefully at the skateboard. I was surprised to see she was interested in it.

"It's high quality." She nodded, still examining it.

"Yeah, that's why it costs almost a hundred bucks. I've saved for months now, but I have only about fifteen dollars. I don't know if I'll ever be able to afford it." I shrugged.

"You will. I'm sure." Sophie grinned, and we kept on walking.

❖　❖　❖

Sophie and I started meeting almost every day by the little patch of grass next to the oak tree. Each time we met, Sophie had a well-planned schedule. We rode my bike from one place to the next with Sophie sitting on a piece of cardboard that I fixed on the back rack for her. She would usually hold the back of the rack or the sides of my seat, but this one time, when we were riding downhill from the library, I suddenly felt her arms wrap around my waist.

I was happy she couldn't see me blush.

We'd ride to the grocery store, and Sophie would buy fruits, vegetables, and types of spices I didn't even know existed. We'd go to the library and talk on the way about what Sophie was reading. When we weren't talking, Sophie would whistle tunes of a kind of music I had never heard before. "Where I come from, the music has quarter tones. That is why it sounds weird to you," she explained when I asked her about it.

After finishing Sophie's daily to-do list, we would sometimes take long walks around the park or in the open fields to the west of our neighborhood. I told her about my childhood, my friends, and about my parents.

My father, Paul, worked at a bus company as an accountant. He left every morning before I woke up. He didn't like his job and was mostly interested in reading his evening newspaper and watching his baseball team on TV. We didn't talk much, but every Sunday afternoon, we would walk together to the park and play catch with the baseball glove he'd given me for my birthday. The previous Christmas he'd bought me a baseball signed by his favorite pitcher and had gotten emotional when he gave it to me.

My dad didn't get emotional often, but I remember that once, when he told me about his teenage years and how his father had thrown away his drum set when he threatened to leave the house and join a touring band, his eyes began tearing up.

My mother, Annie, worked as a secretary at city hall. She loved her job but hated the mayor in office. His name was Joe Triolesta, and he'd served as the mayor for the last four years. He was an older man who had been a successful businessman. My father liked him because he "takes care of business and helps reduce taxes." My mother thought differently, however. She complained that Joe Triolesta didn't care about workers or the poor people in our town, and she and my dad argued about this frequently.

My mother also had a serious problem with cleaning. Everything had to be spotless and squeaky-clean all the time. She would clean the house over and over, saying germs were dangerous and disgusting. She ironed her clothes for an hour before getting dressed every morning. Everything had to be perfect.

The funny thing was that she smoked all the time, one cigarette after another, so the house was clean but smelled like an ashtray.

Sophie asked a lot of questions and wanted to know everything about me. It felt good to have someone so interested in me, my thoughts, and my feelings. Sophie and I got a little closer every day.

From time to time, my bike buddies rode past us, making not-so-funny comments about my being with Sophie all the time, but I didn't care. Being with Sophie was much more interesting than riding around with them, looking for trouble.

"Picking up another physics book?" I asked her one afternoon as we walked into our town's public library.

"No. I'm reading about philosophy now," she replied, putting the book she'd finished back in the return box.

"Isn't philosophy about old Greek guys in white robes? Sounds boring to me." I smirked.

Mrs. Milgram, the librarian, waved to Sophie with a smile. Sophie was probably her most loyal customer.

"You're wrong about philosophy, Leo. It's not boring at all." Sophie was looking around. "I need to find that book. It's funny, but *it is* about an old Greek guy—his name was Aristotle. He's the father of logic and science." She turned to walk toward the philosophy section in the back of the library.

I went to the comic book section. It had been a while since I'd looked through the magazines there.

And there it was: a new comic book by David Brankow, my favorite artist. I grabbed it, sat down on the floor, and started reading.

I thought Orthea was the most beautiful comic book character ever made. She had green, cat-like eyes and wore a black outfit that covered her whole body and face. This was the second volume about Orthea's struggle to free her kingdom, and I dove into the story, turning page after page until Sophie's voice snapped me back to reality.

"She is so beautiful." I looked up to see Sophie standing over me and quickly closed the book.

"What happened? Why did you stop reading?" Sophie asked curiously.

"Nothing. You startled me—that's all."

Sophie's smile widened as she reached for the book. "Can I see it?"

"Nope." I moved it away from her, hiding it behind my back.

"Why? It looks beautiful. What's wrong?"

"I don't know. It's just that…that I always read it by myself." I didn't have any reasonable explanation.

Sophie squatted with her back against the wall next to me. "I like you, Leo." She smiled. "Even though you're a little too shy about how much you love this kind of art."

Sophie was close to me, and I looked at her lips as she smiled softly. I turned back to the book.

"I like you too, Soph," I said quietly, not looking at her, "even though you're asking too many questions."

She giggled, and it made me feel better. I moved closer to her and re-opened the comic book. We were sitting close, our shoulders touching, as I explained the whole *Legacy of Celestia* story to her. By the time we got to Orthea, I was really excited.

"Orthea is the princess of the Celestia Kingdom. She's a princess by day and a spy by night. She tries to save the empire by gathering intelligence and feeding it to the Celestia army general—anonymously, of course." I made sure not to miss a single detail.

I explained to Sophie why I thought Orthea was a fantastic character and why her black-leather costume was a work of art.

"Look how he drew the leather around her body. See this line that goes all the way from her shoulders through the waistline, down to her feet? See how it connects to those elastic, black-leather shoes so seamlessly?"

I turned to see Sophie beaming.

"What?" I stopped.

"Nothing. Please continue; this is fascinating." Sophie seemed pleased about something.

"What is it?" I insisted. Sophie started laughing, holding her hand to her mouth and trying her best not to make too much noise.

"Wait...what?" I started giggling myself at Sophie's attempts to keep it down. Then, because Sophie was covering her mouth, she let out a snort that sent both of us to the floor, rolling with laughter.

"Shush!" Mrs. Milgram called from her desk.

It took us a minute to calm down. We sat next to each other with our backs leaning against the wall.

"Why did you laugh? I still don't get it," I said as I picked up the comic book from the floor.

"It's just great to see how much you enjoy this." She smiled and rested her chin on the tip of my shoulder. I could feel her breath on my neck, and my heart started racing.

"It's just a comic book." I thought of something quick to say.

"Yes, just a comic book." She lifted her head.

"Oh, shut up," I said, shoving her shoulder gently with mine. I was disappointed I couldn't find something smarter to say while Sophie was resting her chin on my shoulder. I stood up, returned the comic book to its shelf, and we exited the library.

On the way back home, Sophie told me about the philosophy book she'd started reading. She was carrying it under her arm. "It's fascinating. It talks about what makes us human. Do you know what makes us human, Leo?" She turned to me, looking like she knew the answer to an important question.

"We can think, and we can talk," I answered.

"Precisely," Sophie said, pointing her finger at me.

"You're reading too much. Where are you getting those words from?" I smirked.

"Listen, did you ever think what words *are*?" Sophie often asked these peculiar questions about seemingly obvious things.

"What do you mean? We use them to talk to each other." I turned to look at her, smirking.

"Yes, but there is something else about them. Words allow us to think, and they are so powerful because each one is a concept. You can say 'bicycle,' and I immediately know what you mean. And the word 'bicycle' means any type of bicycle ever made, in any color or any size. Words shrink the whole universe right into our heads. It blows my mind," she said, waving her hand in the air.

I'd never met anyone who could get so excited about those kinds of things.

"As I said, you got the too-many-books syndrome." I shook my head.

"Well, you love stories. I happen to love ideas. That's it. And speaking of stories—Orthea symbolizes something for you, doesn't she?" Sophie was looking downward. It looked like she was thinking about something but didn't want to say it.

She was right. Orthea *did* mean something special to me.

"She does." I nodded. "She is such a perfect character. I even dreamed about her once."

Sophie didn't say anything. We just walked for a minute, silently, as we got closer to our neighborhood.

"I think you'll be an animator or some kind of an artist when you grow up." Sophie raised her head and looked at me.

It was the first time the option of art as a profession had crossed my mind. It was so profound that I felt the idea seeping deep into my mind, making me feel like life was suddenly full of possibilities.

"So you've learned all that from this philosophy book?" I asked as we descended toward the road that led to our neighborhood.

"Yes, and much more. You know how when you buy something new, it comes with instructions?"

I nodded. "Like a user manual."

"Right. Well, I think of philosophy as a manual for life," she said, tapping the book she was holding. "I think everyone should read philosophy."

I turned around and started walking backward down the hill, facing Sophie. "How about you read it and give me the highlights?"

"I'll try." Sophie chuckled.

We turned left and entered our neighborhood. Sophie's brown house still looked like no one was living in it. Some of the shutters were missing, and some were broken. It seemed old, and I felt sorry for Sophie.

We stopped by its gate.

"I'm sorry I can't invite you in. My mother isn't feeling well, and she is too weak to have any visitors," Sophie said.

"It's fine, Soph. Don't worry about it." I shrugged.

"I'll see you tomorrow." She smiled and turned to walk up the stairs to the brown house's wooden front deck.

Just as I was about to walk away, I heard a door opening and a loud cough. I turned and saw a woman wearing a long black gown and a scarf. She was standing and then bent over, coughing loudly.

She straightened, looking at Sophie and then at me. Her face was white, and the black scarf covered part of her mouth. It seemed like all I could see was a pair of big green, cat-like eyes that stared straight at me for a long moment without blinking. For a brief second, I was lost in the depth of those eyes, but then I took a step back, swiftly got on my bike, and pedaled away.

Holy moly! Sophie's mom is a living version of Orthea, I thought, pedaling fast. I couldn't decide if I felt guilty for turning away from Sophie and her mother so abruptly or confused over why the heck I'd done that.

CHAPTER 3

NUNU

The next day I waited for Sophie near our oak tree as usual. She wasn't there.

I walked up to her house and stood by the gate. I started walking back and forth from one side of the brown house's fence to the other. The front yard held several citrus trees—the same ones the Draculas had protected so fiercely from the developers building our neighborhood and from the kids' baseballs and soccer balls. An old tin shed sat to the side of the garden, and I noticed a little, well-kept flowerbed closer to the house. It contained several green plants that looked like herbs.

After waiting for a while, I started thinking that maybe Sophie's mother, the woman with Orthea's eyes, had seen something in me and decided Sophie should never hang out with me again.

I went back home, worried.

Later that evening, as I sat in my room drawing, I heard something hit my bedroom window. When I looked out, I saw Sophie looking up at me. She had wood chips in one hand, and she was just about to throw another piece with the other. She stopped and lowered her hand when she realized I was looking out the window.

It was getting dark, but I could still see her face. I immediately knew something was wrong. The spark in Sophie's eyes was missing. I did my "firefighter drill" and climbed, legs first, out the window, stepping carefully onto the black shingles of the porch's roof and then sliding from one of the porch poles down to the ground.

"Hey, is everything OK?" I asked as I got closer.

Sophie looked at me and, without saying anything, turned and started walking back to the trail that led to the neighborhood park. I followed her.

A gentle, cool breeze moved the leaves in the trees above us as we sat beneath our oak tree's branches. It was quiet, and I waited patiently for Sophie to tell me what was going on. It seemed like she needed the time.

"My grandfather died last night," she said. "He died back in Syria."

As she raised her head to look at me, I could see her eyes tearing up. She sat on one of the oak tree's exposed roots, her knees pulled up to her chest, her arms wrapped around them. We sat there for a couple of minutes in silence as the wind started blowing a little harder. Sophie was wearing a thin, short-sleeved shirt and looked cold. I took off my hoodie and covered her shoulders with it.

"Were you close to him?" I asked, breaking the silence.

Sophie nodded. She lowered her head, resting her forehead on her knees. I was sad to see her like this.

I thought about my grandfather, who had died when I was only four years old. I had vague memories of how he looked—nothing more. We had a picture of him and my grandmother, who had passed away many years before him, on a shelf above the fireplace. My mother told me he had been a talented painter but hadn't been able to practice his art; he'd had to work as a traveling salesperson to make a living. One of his landscape drawings decorated the hall on the way to my bedroom. I often stopped and looked at the painting's subtle details—the light at the edges of leaves on the trees, the different grass types, and the thin haze above a distant mountain ridge. It was beautiful, and every time I dove into that painting, I found something new I hadn't noticed before.

Sophie sniffed quietly, but it was enough to snap me out of thoughts about my own grandfather.

"So you're from Syria?" I tried to recall where I had seen that country's name on the world map I had on my bedroom wall.

"Yes. That's where I'm from. Or actually...where I escaped from." Sophie looked at me as if to see how I would react.

"*Escaped?* Why did you escape? Did something happen?"

"A lot happened. My grandfather was a university professor in Damascus, the capital of Syria. He wrote articles against the government and got into a lot of trouble for it. You're not supposed to do that."

"What do you mean, 'You're not supposed to do that'? I don't understand." I was confused.

"You see, here in the United States, people take things for granted—like freedom of speech. Here you can say whatever you want, even if it offends people. That's what's so great about this place and why I love it so much. But you cannot imagine what it means to live in a place where you have to think about every word you say—anyone can report you to the government at any time, and people sometimes just...disappear." Sophie stopped and wiped her cheek with the back of her hand.

"I didn't know that's how things are over there," I admitted.

"Well, it is," Sophie said, and her voice broke. She covered her face with her arm, and her head moved up and down as she was sobbing faintly.

It took her a minute to calm down.

"I remember he used to take me down to his basement library," she said, gazing up at the dark sky. "It was a big, stuffed room with a heavy smell of old books. He would hold my hand, wander around the shelves, pick a book, sit me down on his lap, and read it to me. He was such a gentle person. It was like he knew everything and had an answer to any question I could come up with. He taught me English when I was very young and watched old western movies with me. You know what he used to do? He would put tape on the TV to hide the subtitles."

"Sounds like he was a smart guy," I smiled.

"Yes, he was." Sophie sounded a bit better. "He taught philosophy and students loved him. He was an expert in ancient Greek philosophy and Aristotle was his hero."

"Well, that explains a lot," I said, and Sophie raised her head and smiled at me.

"And what about your father?" I asked. "Where is he?" Sophie never mentioned him.

"My father..." Sophie paused and then took a long, deep breath. "Well, my father is very different from my grandfather. You see, my grandfather was a man of thought, and my father is a man of action. They used to argue all the time. Last year, my father started an underground movement to fight Syria's dictator and his corrupt government. But soon after, one of the members snitched on them to the secret service, and they caught him and most of the other underground members. Last we heard from him, he was being kept in a jail somewhere in the south. He is probably dead by now." Sophie's face contorted with pain, and a single tear rolled from her eye to the edge of her nose. It hung there for a quick moment before falling and disappearing into the grass below.

"I'm sorry, Soph," I said and reached my hand out to her. Sophie looked at me and slowly extended her hand. She rested the palm of her hand over mine, and I squeezed it lightly.

Sophie looked at me, her eyebrows drawn together. There was no sadness in her eyes, only that piercing look that had made me uncomfortable the first time I'd met her. She had this tendency of looking straight at me in moments that felt a little awkward. And for some strange reason, instead of feeling even more awkward, it made me feel good as if things were honest and open between us.

I was thinking about her mother and how she reminded me of Orthea. Sophie had the same intense eyes, but hers were black or a brown so dark you couldn't see the difference between her pupils and her iris.

Sophie turned to face me while still holding my hand. "I remember the last time I saw him," she said. "He was arguing with my grandfather. They were in the basement, and I sneaked to the top of the basement staircase so I could hear what they were saying. That argument was more intense than usual. My grandfather threatened to disown him if he went ahead with his plan. 'Revolutions start with ideas, not brute force. You won't have the support you'll need,' he told him. My dad called him a coward and stormed out of the room. He saw me at the top of the stairs. He stopped next to me, brushed his hand through my hair, and stormed out of the house. They caught him three weeks later, and after that happened, my grandfather immediately sent us to Europe on the first flight out. And from Europe, we came to the US."

Sophie looked around at the dark, empty park around us. The wind was now blowing even harder, and all we could hear were the leaves rustling in the wind and crickets chirping from the grassland in the middle of the park.

"Let's walk. I'm getting cold sitting here." Sophie stood quickly as she snapped out of the gloomy mood she'd been in a second ago. She handed me my hoodie.

"Keep it. It's cold," I said, but Sophie wouldn't. I took back the hoodie but didn't put it on. I tied it around my waist and started walking back toward my house.

"You know what I used to call my grandfather?" Sophie's mouth curved into a smile as we exited the park.

"What?" I asked.

"Nunu. And my grandmother's nickname was Nuna. She died when I was three and a half years old. I hardly remember her, but I do remember her long white hair. She came from a rich family, and she met Nunu in France when they were both students. My father was their only child."

Sophie was grinning, and I was happy to see she was feeling better.

"He used to wire us some money every month. Now I don't know what we're going to do. And I don't know where I'm going to get the money to—" Sophie stopped in the middle of the sentence.

"What?" I asked. I turned to her. "Get money for what?"

Sophie stared at me for a couple of seconds. She was thinking hard about something and looked like she was trying to decide whether to tell me about it.

"What is it, Soph?" I got a little closer to her.

"It has to be a secret, Leo," she whispered. She looked at the ground.

"Of course—you know I won't tell anyone," I whispered back.

Sophie bent over and picked a blade of grass from the lawn we were walking across. She started rolling it between her thumb and finger and then turned to face me again.

"I'm not an American citizen," she said. "People have to have a visa in order to stay here. We did have one, but it expired a while back. That's why we had to move from the big city when people started to get suspicious. I thought that here it would be less risky, but if we get caught, we could be deported back to Syria." Sophie paused. "And if that happens, I don't think we will be able to make it out from there again."

I looked at her. Sophie's face was calm and relaxed, which amazed me, considering what she'd just shared.

"Wow," I finally blurted.

"Yeah, interesting situation, isn't it? There is a lawyer who can find a way to keep us here, but he's asking for a lot of money." She sniffled and started walking toward the bike track that circled the lawn in the middle of the park. We were halfway between my house and hers.

"How much is he asking for?" I asked.

"Five thousand dollars for the whole process. So I'm saving as much as I can."

"Can he get you a visa? Will that make you a citizen?" I was hoping there was a solution to all this.

"Sort of. He can change our immigration status, which will allow us to stay here." Sophie nodded. "But it's five thousand dollars. I've paid him three thousand so far, which was everything I've managed to save from the allowance we got every month from my grandfather. But now...I don't know."

"It'll be fine, Soph. I won't let them deport you," I reassured her without knowing how I could actually keep a promise like that.

Her face brightened. She walked toward me and gave me a quick hug that was over before I was able to react.

"Good night, Leo. And thank you," Sophie said. She turned around to walk back to her house.

"Don't mention it," I replied.

I watched her walk away, and I headed home, beating myself up for not hugging her back. *How stupid of me*, I thought as I climbed the balcony's roof back to my window, which I'd left open.

I sat on the wooden chair in front of my desk, feeling worried about Sophie but also a little happy—it was the first hug I'd ever received from a girl. I took my sketch pad from my desk drawer and drew a new character for a story that had swirled in my head for a couple of days.

CHAPTER 4

THE BULLY

The days were long, hot, and humid, but I loved every minute of summer break. I had fun spending time with Sophie, and I wasn't looking forward to going back to school.

Sophie and I liked to walk down to the small creek that passed a mile south of our neighborhood and cool our feet in the water. On a Friday afternoon, just before school started, Sophie made me carry a watermelon all the way to the creek. She also brought a little bag and wouldn't let me see what was inside.

"Trust me—you'll love it," she said when I asked for an explanation.

"This thing is heavy," I complained when I picked the watermelon up. Sophie frowned at me with a half smile.

"What?" I said. "Can't a guy complain a little?"

"No. Now come on. Let's go," She turned her head toward the road that led to the neighborhood's south exit.

When we got there, Sophie took out a little blanket. She laid it on the ground in the shade of a tree that stood right on the waterfront. After we sat down, she took out a knife and cut the watermelon into perfectly even slices. Then she cut the watermelon pieces into triangles and placed them in a plastic bowl she took out of her bag.

"Cool," I said and reached for a slice.

Sophie slapped my hand and shook her head. "Patience, kid."

I smiled and crossed my hands, looking at her as she took a round pack of feta cheese and crumbled a piece of it over the watermelon.

"What are you doing? You're ruining the watermelon," I grumbled. "That's salty stuff."

"Try it," she said, handing me a slice with some cheese on it. The sweetness of the watermelon and the saltiness of the cheese blended in a way I hadn't expected. It was good, and I was surprised two things I would never think would go together actually did.

I smiled and took another piece. Sophie looked pleased and lowered her head onto the blanket, closing her eyes. I lay back down as well, resting on my elbows as I looked around. It was quiet, and all I could hear were the sounds of the water flowing slowly down the stream and faint chirping of birds from the other side of the creek. I felt relaxed and happy. I thought that if I could stop time from moving forward, I would do it right now.

But I couldn't, and school was starting Monday. Suddenly, a thought crossed my mind.

"Wait." I turned to Sophie. "Aren't you going to have a problem going to school if you're illegal? They can report you to the police, can't they?"

"No, I've checked it," Sophie said, lifting herself. "There is this Supreme Court ruling that says that kids of illegal immigrants can go to school without being reported. They didn't ask for my social security number or anything when I went with my mother to register, so I don't think I'll have a problem. Last year, in the other city we lived in, I stayed home, and even though I loved teaching myself things by reading books, it was hard to be so isolated. I'm totally looking forward to starting school."

"So how long are you in the US? And how did you get *here* from all places?" I asked.

"We landed eleven months ago in New York, and we stayed there in a little apartment. It was cold during the winter, and the air wasn't good for my mother. So we decided to move. And with our immigration issue, I thought that a remote place like this one would be best."

"You mean, a place in the middle of nowhere," I chuckled. Sophie laughed gaily, and I took another piece of the feta and watermelon.

❖　❖　❖

Monday morning, on the first day of school, I met Sophie next to our old oak tree.

"We're in the same class!" I cheered as I got closer to her. "I didn't see you at the orientation last night, but we're both in Mrs. Ripley's class!"

"Great!" Sophie exclaimed. She lifted herself from leaning on the tree's trunk and walked toward me, smiling. I had my new backpack hanging over my shoulder and noticed Sophie had a plastic grocery bag with a couple of books and a pencil in it.

We started walking and turned left out of our neighborhood toward the school, which was about ten minutes away. On the way there, we passed the strip mall that had the grocery store we visited often, some restaurants, and a large office building.

Mrs. Ripley didn't turn out to be the best teacher, to say the least. She was old, never smiled, and was short-tempered. She had gray hair and a pair of pointed-frame glasses with a thin metal chain that made her look like an angry grandmother. "Two more years until my retirement, and honestly...I can't wait," she said to us during the first lesson we had with her that day.

I introduced Sophie to most of the kids in class: to Chloe, the girl who sat next to me; to Sarah, the girl with the round glasses who was taking pictures all day with her camera; and to Chris, Jordan, and Brian, who were part of my bike squad.

By the end of the first week of school, Sophie knew almost everyone. I saw her talking to David and Daniel, the nerdy twins, and even to Big Frankie, whom we called "TM," which stood for Troublemaker.

When she talked to them, she asked questions about what they liked and their hobbies, and that got some of them talking. Daniel, for example, explained to her everything he knew about airplanes and the models he collected.

That same day, right after lunch, as we walked out to the hall, Sophie met Nancy Sanders. Nancy was standing with two girls on the other side of the wide corridor. All three of them stared at Sophie, who was walking in front of me.

As Sophie passed by them, Nancy gave her a condescending smirk and said, "Your parents can't afford a new dress?"

The girls giggled and walked away.

Sophie stopped for a moment but then continued to walk toward the hall exit as if nothing had happened. I watched Nancy and the two girls as they blended with other groups of students down the hallway.

I wanted to run toward Nancy and do something but decided against it.

Nancy Sanders was the most popular girl in our grade. I'd met her when we started elementary school together. She was always in the middle of everything; she was on student council and all kinds of school committees. Teachers treated her nicely, and I guessed this was because of her family—Nancy's grandfather was the state governor, and her mother was the famous Ingrid Sanders, who was running for mayor and also was the chairwoman of our school's board.

I didn't like Nancy, but other kids thought she was going to be a very important person one day. She probably thought so too.

The year before, Nancy had come up with an idea to stop students from talking during lunch, because she thought they made too much noise, and some never got to finish their food on time. She passed a rule with student council that during the first ten minutes of lunchtime, music would play and students would not be allowed to talk. Teachers loved it, but the rest of us hated it.

"It's good for you. You'll thank me one day," Nancy explained to those who complained about it.

I walked outside but couldn't find Sophie anywhere. When it was time for the next period, Sophie entered the classroom just a second before Mr. Sumner, our science teacher, walked in. She sat in the back row of the class, and as she passed me on her way there, I looked up at her. I expected her to be upset or to see traces of tears in her eyes, but instead, her face was calm and relaxed, and she walked slowly and confidently to the back of the class.

On the way back from school, we didn't say a word.

Days and weeks went by, and each morning Sophie and I met next to the oak tree and walked to school together. Sophie would usually hold a library book with her index finger stuck in the middle of it, acting as a bookmark.

Sophie didn't participate much during classes. From time to time, when I looked back at her, sitting in the back row, I would notice a book resting on her lap.

The only class Sophie enjoyed was science. I think it was because of Mr. Sumner, who was young, tall and liked by most girls in our class. He had blond hair, and he wore funky clothes. He showed up to school in colorful shirts, pants, and even shoes.

"Science is a mystery, and we are detectives," he said at the beginning of every class. Everyone thought he was great; I thought he was way too nice.

As weeks passed by, autumn slowly colored our oak tree a fiery orange. Later, winter plucked it naked of its leaves.

One cold Monday, just before midterms, Sophie and I sat outside for lunch on a long concrete bench that surrounded the school's backyard. We were just about ready to start eating our sandwiches. I had a blue tin lunch box with an embossed Spiderman figure that I really liked. Spiderman was in his red-and-blue suit on a skyscraper's roof, crouching with one hand on the floor and shooting white webs from the other. I had tried copying the pose on paper many times, trying to get the proportions right.

Sophie had a red apple and a sandwich wrapped in a white napkin. As Sophie took the first bite of her apple, I noticed Emmanuel and his gang walking toward us.

At least a head taller than Big Frankie, Emmanuel was a big kid from our class. His nickname was "Manu," and he often got in trouble for starting fights—fights in which he did most of the hitting.

I rose to my feet, picking up my lunch box. I didn't like Emmanuel and tried to stay out of his way. Sophie remained sitting, eating her apple and looking up at me as if she didn't understand why I was on my feet. I guess she didn't know Emmanuel well enough, but I'd seen him and his friends looking for trouble before, and now it was coming my way.

I was nervous. A couple of seconds later, Emmanuel was right in front of me. He stopped an inch from my nose and was staring me down. He looked down at Sophie, who was still sitting, chewing her apple.

"Nice lunch box," he said, laughing as he looked down at the tin lunch box in my right hand.

I said nothing. Emmanuel's face was so close to mine that I stopped breathing.

"Guys, did you see the Spiderman on this thing?" He turned to his three friends, who stood behind him wearing foolish grins of anticipation.

"Have you kept that since kindergarten or what?" He snorted as he turned to face me again, and the three kids behind him burst into laughter.

We stood there for a couple of seconds, looking at each other. Suddenly, Emmanuel reached out to snatch the lunch box from my hand. I pulled it back before he could reach it.

"Leave me alone, Manu," I hissed in the most threatening tone I could come up with.

Emmanuel grinned. He took another quick look back at his friends. Swiftly, he turned back to me, grabbed the lunch box with one hand, and pushed hard against my chest with the other. I was not ready for that push and completely lost my balance. I fell backward, the backs of my knees buckled against the ramp, throwing my body back until my head smacked the flat concrete.

I felt a sharp pain in the back of my head, and I could feel it swelling rapidly. I was stunned for a couple of seconds, and I slowly sat up with my eyes closed, holding my head with both my hands.

I heard a noise and opened my eyes. I saw Sophie stalking after Emmanuel, who had started walking toward the school building with his friends. When she caught up to him, she stood right in front of him, blocking his way.

I stood and started walking toward them, still holding the back of my head, which was pounding with pain.

"Get out of my way, little girl," Emmanuel snarled, looking down at Sophie. "That is if you want to get back home in one piece to play with your dolls."

I got closer and stopped to Emmanuel's left, looking at Sophie, who was still staring right at him. Sophie didn't move, and Emmanuel was smiling. He turned to his friends with his arms raised to his sides as if to ask, "What do I do with this girl?"

"Move," he said finally, turning back to Sophie with a threatening look.

Sophie didn't move.

"I said *move!*" he shouted, moving a step closer to her. Sophie had to look up at Emmanuel, who was now a few inches from her. Her eyes were fixed on him with a piercing stare, her eyebrows drawn together in a serious look.

They stood there staring at each other for a few seconds, while the three kids started teasing Emmanuel for not doing anything about the situation.

"Are you going to make her move or what?" the shortest of the three asked, chuckling.

Emmanuel dropped my lunch box to the ground and moved his entire body forward, shoving Sophie hard with both hands. Sophie's thin body flew up in the air and then down to the ground, her back hitting the dirt.

Sophie quickly pushed herself up, sitting for a quick second in the dirt before pulling herself up to a stand. She walked back to the same spot she'd been standing in a couple of seconds ago, right in front of Emmanuel.

"Unbelievable." Emmanuel chuckled and immediately pushed her again. This time he used a downward motion, sending Sophie to the ground right beneath him. Sophie stood and faced Emmanuel once again, standing even closer to him than before.

Emmanuel's face changed. It was like he had run out of ideas. Sophie was now staring him down—not the other way around.

Emmanuel's friends and I watched all this, not moving or saying anything.

Other kids started getting closer, trying to see what was going on. Very quickly, we had a circle of kids around us, while Sophie and Emmanuel were still staring at each other.

Suddenly, Sophie started talking, silencing the murmur around us.

"So that's who you are? A petty thief? A bully?" Sophie's voice was clear and loud.
"I've been watching you, Manu. I think you're smart; I even think you're creative and funny—that's how you get to lead your little group here, right?" Sophie tilted her head toward his three friends, who looked at them silently, as did the other kids in the circle around Sophie and Emmanuel.

"But for some reason, you don't think that being smart is cool, and you spend your time doing senseless things like taking other kids' lunch boxes. I think you can do better than that, don't you?"

Emmanuel was confused. He was aware of the growing circle of kids looking at him, and for the first time, it seemed he was at a loss for words.

"You don't want to be a thief; thieves live miserable lives, and because they know they didn't earn the things they take from other people, they end up destroying themselves. Is that what you want for yourself? Because I think you can do better!" Sophie paused.

Emmanuel didn't move and was just staring down at her, looking confused. He surely hadn't expected this. Sophie continued, sounding even more confident. "Stealing is for cowards, Emmanuel, and you're not a coward; I know you're not."

"Wh...what?" Emmanuel was baffled.

Sophie didn't waste time. "Look, you don't need Leo's dry peanut butter sandwich." Sophie pointed at the Spiderman lunch box lying on the ground. "And you know what? I'll make you a deal—I'll make sure you get an A on next week's math test, and you stop wasting your time pushing kids around. What do you say?" Sophie raised her head a little higher and looked him straight in the eye, extending her hand toward him for a handshake. "I'll meet you at the library tomorrow after school. Deal?"

Emmanuel looked around, ignoring Sophie's extended hand. He looked at the skinny kid from his three-member gang. The kid raised his shoulders and shook his head; he didn't have any ideas for Emmanuel.

Emmanuel squatted, picked up my lunch box, and turned back to look at Sophie. He raised his chin a little, standing up straight again. Sophie lowered her hand.

"I'm full anyway." Emmanuel turned and threw the lunch box at me. I was startled but still managed to catch it.

"Come on, guys. Let's go," he said to his friends.

As they walked back to the entrance of the school, I noticed Emmanuel turning back to look at Sophie, who was still standing there, watching him.

When Emmanuel and his friends entered the school hall, the circle of kids around us dispersed.

Sophie turned to me. "Are you OK?" she asked. She leaned over to look at the lump at the back of my head. "You'll need to put some ice on that."

"I'll be fine." I shrugged and turned to pick up my backpack. Sophie followed me, and we walked back to the school building. On our way there, I noticed Sophie's hands were trembling.

"You didn't have to do this. I can take care of myself, you know," I said.

"I know you can. And I didn't do it for you. I did it for myself." Sophie opened the door and went into the school's main hall. I stopped, holding the open door, puzzled by Sophie's answer. I stood looking at her as her slim figure got smaller in the depth of the big hall. I didn't understand what she meant.

Emmanuel met Sophie every afternoon for the rest of the week in the school's library. The following week, he got his first A ever on the math midterm, and needless to say, he and his gang never bothered us again.

CHAPTER 5

HIDDEN FORCE

A cold winter break had passed, and we started school again.

"Ms. Anwar—Sophia Anwar?" Ms. White, our school secretary, came running out of the front office as Sophie and I passed by on our way to class. Ms. White moved in small, clacking steps in her high-heeled shoes. She was tall and blond and always had this smile on her face that looked like it had nothing to do with what she was saying. She reminded me of a Barbie doll with a permanent plastic smile.

We both turned to her as she got closer to us.

"At two thirty I need you to be at the front office, dear. There is a committee meeting you need to attend."

"What kind of committee?" Sophie asked.

"It's a..." The secretary glanced at me for a quick second. "It's a social committee with our school principal, our social worker, and a representative from the school board."

"What is it about?" Sophie continued to inquire with her eyebrows drawn together, looking suspicious.

"I...I don't really know. Just be at the front office at OK, dear?" Ms. White didn't wait for an answer and hurrie office, avoiding any additional questions.

At half past two, instead of going back home, I walked with Sophie to the front office. Ms. White greeted Sophie with a wider smile than usual, which looked like it made Sophie even more suspicious and uncomfortable. I could see it from the two wrinkles at the edges of her eyebrows, which popped up every time she was thinking about something serious.

"Leo, the meeting is for Sophie only," Ms. White nodded to me gently.

"I know, I'll just wait for her outside," I replied.

"They will see you in a couple of minutes," said Ms. White and turned to Sophie. She pointed to the bench to the left of the office door. Sophie and I sat on it and waited.

Then Ingrid Sanders walked in.

Mrs. Sanders was very well-known in our town and was involved with every committee in city hall and in several public schools, including ours. She had run for mayor in the previous election but had lost to old Mayor Triolesta. The next election was taking place later that year, and Mrs. Sanders had started campaigning against Joe Triolesta. My mother, who worked in one of the offices in city hall, said Ingrid Sanders would do anything to get elected this time around.

The Sanders family lived in a big house just down the road from the big church. People talked about their flashy lifestyle and fancy cars, and some id there had to be something fishy about them—they didn't have a ranch and didn't produce anything to justify their wealth.

"A family of politicians. That says it all," my father said, but I didn't understand what he meant by that.

My mother knew Ingrid well and invited her over to our house from time to time after church. Even though my mother formally worked for the current mayor, she hoped Mrs. Sanders would win. She was always excited before Mrs. Sanders came over and would clean the house for hours before every visit.

Ms. White stood to greet her. Mrs. Sanders wore a gray skirt suit and a thin white scarf. She waved and smiled at Ms. White with lips that seemed perfectly drawn with red lipstick. She looked as though she had come out of a Hollywood movie scene or some fashion magazine. Mrs. Sanders stopped to talk to Ms. White for a quick moment.

Sophie and I were both staring at Ingrid Sanders as she nodded to Ms. White and then walked slowly and elegantly into the boardroom.

"She looks like an older version of Nancy." I chuckled, but Sophie didn't smile.

As she entered the boardroom, we heard Mrs. Sanders greeting Mr. Palmer, our school principal, and another woman sitting next to him. I knew the woman worked at our school—I'd seen her before—but didn't know who she was.

The boardroom had a big window that faced the back of the school, and I could see through the open door that it was slightly open.

Sophie sat beside me, watching the three people in the room carefully. Her hands were on her lap, calm and relaxed, holding her plastic bag. Ms. White nodded to Sophie to walk into the room.

As soon as the door closed, without thinking much, I ran around to the back of the building until I got to the boardroom's window that was open. It was conveniently low, and I could easily see and hear what was happening in the room. I sat below the window ledge so no one could see me.

"Sophia Anwar?" I heard Mr. Palmer ask in his friendly voice.

"Yes. That's me, but you can call me Sophie," Sophie replied confidently.

"Very well, Sophie. This is Ms. Adams, our school social worker, and this is Mrs. Sanders, the head of our school board. The reason we invited you, Sophie, is to make sure that everything is well with you and your family. We would like to ask you a couple of questions. All right?"

"I don't know. We'll see," Sophie replied, and I heard Mr. Palmer respond with a titter.

"Sophie, you're here because we couldn't get a hold of your parents." I heard a voice I did not recognize and assumed it was Ms. Adams talking. I knew Mrs. Sanders's voice. It had this deep tone to it, from the cigarettes she was constantly smoking.

"How are things at home, Sophie?" Ms. Adams continued.

"Things are well," Sophie answered briefly.

"Are you getting everything that you need at home? Food, clothes?"

"I am getting everything I need," Sophie answered, and there was a moment of silence. Then Sophie said: "And if you are referring to the fact that my clothes are kind of old, yes, we don't have much money. But last I checked, being poor is not a crime, right?"

I heard Mr. Palmer clearing his throat. "No, no, of course not. That is not what we are asking," he said in an apologetic tone.

"Then why am I here?" Sophie replied immediately, sounding impatient.

How does she do it? How is she not afraid to talk to the school principal this way? I thought as I squatted beneath the window.

"Well, we have a report about a fight that took place in the schoolyard. Can you tell us about what happened there?" Mr. Palmer asked.

"My friend and I were picked on by some other kids, but it's fine. We've settled it." Sophie was brief and sounded like she wasn't interested in talking about it.

"So I hear. You've offered Emmanuel private tutoring, is that right?" Mr. Palmer sounded amused.

"I did, but this whole thing is behind us," Sophie replied. She, unlike Mr. Palmer, didn't find it funny.

"Good," Mr. Palmer concluded.

I raised my head to peek a little to see what was happening in the room. Mr. Palmer was standing with his arms crossed over his chest, and

Ms. Adams and Mrs. Sanders sat with their backs to me. Sophie was sitting on a chair in front of them, not looking too happy.

I lowered my head back below the ledge.

"So why am I here?" Sophie asked again, sounding even more annoyed than before.

"You are here because we need to make sure that you're being taken care of. It's the law," Ms. Adams replied.

"It's the community's duty to make sure you are provided with the things you need as a child and as a student," Mrs. Sanders said in her distinct voice. She was trying to sound gentle and warm like Ms. Adams, but there was a hint of impatience in her voice.

There was another moment of silence.

"Well...as you can see, I'm not missing anything." Sophie sounded serious, almost irritated.

"Sophie, why aren't you joining the field trip next week?" Ms. Adams asked.

"We can't afford it, and it isn't mandatory. That's what the registration form said, so I decided not to register. Is there something wrong with that?" Sophie's voice was sharp and clear.

Mrs. Sanders replied immediately. "Why are you so defensive? We—"

"That is totally fine, Sophie. You don't have to explain," Ms. Adams interrupted Ingrid Sanders midsentence. Mr. Palmer was clearing his throat again.

"Thank you," Sophie said. "Do you have any more questions for me?"

"Where is that accent from? What is your ethnicity, Sophie?" I heard Mrs. Sanders ask.

Silence. I didn't hear anyone speak for about five seconds, only something that sounded like a pen dropping to the floor.

"Do I have to answer that question?" Sophie finally replied.

"Well..." I heard Mr. Palmer start, but immediately Ms. Adams spoke over him.

"No—no, you don't," she said.

"May I leave now?" Sophie asked.

"Yes, I think that will be all," Ms. Adams replied, and it sounded like she was smiling when she said that. I heard the door open and close. Then I heard Mr. Palmer clear his throat yet again.

"Mrs. Sanders, there is a code to those student interviews. I must ask you to respect them," Ms. Adams said impatiently.

"That girl is interesting. Tough and hardheaded," I heard Mrs. Sanders say in a quiet voice. It seemed like she was completely ignoring what Ms. Adams had just said. "She is stubborn and arrogant. She reminds me of myself at her age, you know? That age when you still don't understand how this world really works." Mrs. Sanders was speaking as if she was thinking this to herself. "I don't know where she came from, but we need to keep an eye on her."

"We will surely do that, Mrs. Sanders," Mr. Palmer reassured her.

I raised my head a little and peeked into the room again. They all had their backs to the window. Ingrid Sanders stood, pushing her chair back and getting ready to leave the room. I lowered myself quietly and ran back to the front office, but I wasn't fast enough, and Sophie was already gone.

I started running and saw Sophie walking alone on the sidewalk in the distance. I ran all the way to her and started walking next to her. Sophie didn't turn to look at me. Her thinking wrinkles were showing as she gazed straight into the distance.

We walked silently for several minutes. The sun was out, and we walked on the side of the street that was partly shaded by a row of trees.

"I heard your conversation with the committee," I admitted to her as we passed the strip mall.

"I know. I caught a glimpse of your face through the back window. Found it interesting?" Sophie asked, and I immediately felt embarrassed for overhearing the conversation.

"Sorry, I should've asked your permission to eavesdrop. I was worried about you. I thought that they might have found out about you being illegal here."

"It's OK. I don't mind." Sophie shook her head. We reached the only street with a passenger traffic light on our way from the neighborhood to school. We waited there for a minute for the light to turn green.

After we crossed the road, Sophie asked, "Did you hear what Mrs. Sanders said about the community's duty to take care of me? What do you think about that?"

"I don't know. I think it is nice of her. Why were you so annoyed?" I asked, recalling Sophie's irritated tone of voice.

"Well, I think it is OK for them to check that I'm doing fine, but I don't think that it is the 'community's duty' to take care of me. I don't like that she used the word 'duty.' I think that it is not anyone's duty to take care of me, other than my parents," Sophie exclaimed. Something was profoundly bothering her.

"Why? I think Mrs. Sanders means well, and she wants to help you." I turned to look at Sophie. Her jaw was clenched, and she had a concerned look on her face.

"It might look like that on the face of it, but I don't think it is that simple. I don't trust her." Sophie surprised me with her answer.

What Sophie said didn't make sense to me. I knew Ingrid Sanders—she was famous around town for good reasons. She cared about people and was working hard to make the city help the poor, especially in the eastern neighborhoods. I'd heard all this from my mother, who continuously updated my father on what was going on at city council during dinnertime.

"You don't trust her? Did you know that she made the city feed people who don't have money?" I argued. "She fought and won against Mayor Triolesta in the city council, and now there are those places that serve free food in the eastern neighborhoods. I'm telling you—you're wrong about her." I stopped walking and looked at Sophie expecting an answer or, more specifically, an explanation.

Sophie stopped walking as well. She was standing several feet in front of me and then turned and stepped toward me, her face becoming a little softer.

"She might have good intentions, Leo. But good intentions can still cause a lot of harm if the ideas behind them are wrong." Sophie was standing close to me with her penetrating look directed at me again.

"I still don't understand how you think that what she is doing is harmful or wrong." I squinted at Sophie. She was still standing close, her eyes piercing.

"It is something I learned from my grandfather—every time force is used, it is harmful to—" Sophie started to explain, but I had to stop her.

"Force? Who's using force? What are you talking about?" I was getting impatient.

"Wait." Sophie raised her hand. "Let's think about this together, Leo. I'm not interested in fighting; I'm interested in understanding this better, OK?"

Sophie has a strange way of approaching things, I thought. "OK, so go ahead; explain it to me," I replied, trying to stay calm.

"All right, I'll try. Who do you think is paying for the food that the city is giving the people in the eastern neighborhoods?" she asked with a tight voice, which made me a little nervous.

"The city," I answered.

"And where does the city get its money from?" Sophie continued as I crossed my arms over my chest.

"Hmm...taxes?" I wasn't sure.

"And do your parents have a choice not to pay taxes?"

"Hmm...no, they have to pay."

"Or else?"

"I don't know. They can go to jail, I guess." I shrugged.

"See? If we dig a little deeper, we find that what's actually happening is that the city *forces* people to pay it money. Otherwise, they'll go to jail. So, the force is there, threatening, even if it's hidden." Sophie was moving her hands while she talked.

"I think that the people who make the money should decide how to spend it, not politicians like Ingrid Sanders—even if the money is spent on helping a poor girl like me." Sophie's voice got soft, and she took a step back.

I didn't know what to say.

"And besides," she added, "getting stuff for free doesn't really help. It makes people lazy and needy. I don't need their help." Sophie turned and started walking away.

It was one of those moments when I just wanted to shout something back but held myself, knowing that it might be better to just shut up and think about it for a minute. There was something about Sophie that made me control myself in a way that I had never before with anyone else.

I caught up with her, but we didn't say another word for the rest of the day.

The winter months passed slowly, and spring, my favorite time of year, came along. Sophie didn't mention it, but I knew money had started becoming a real issue. When we went together to buy some groceries, I noticed she counted the number of apples and chose ones that were a little smaller.

The next morning, we met next to our tree as usual. As I got closer to Sophie, I saw her leaning on the tree's trunk, reading a big, thick book. She didn't lift her eyes from the book, even as I got pretty close to her. She was in that bubble again. Her eyes were rapidly moving back and forth through the lines on the page in front of her. *Introduction to Computer Programming* read the title of the book.

"So you're into computers?" I asked.

"Oh." Sophie looked up at me, a little startled. "I didn't see you coming." She giggled and closed the book.

We started walking, and Sophie put the book in her plastic bag.

"I'm staying at school this afternoon for a computer class. I saw a note on the school message board that a retired computer scientist is giving free lessons." Sophie sounded excited.

"Oh, I know that guy," I said. "It's Mr. Friedman. He lives at the edge of the neighborhood."

I looked down and saw that the sole of Sophie's shoe was coming off, separating at the front. It made it look like the shoe had a mouth. I felt terrible knowing she probably didn't have the money to buy a new pair.

So the next morning, on our way to school, I took out a small pack of bills and handed it to her. I'd saved fifteen dollars and decided she needed it more than I did.

"What is this?" Sophie asked with a serious look on her face.

"I saved up some money, and when you told me about your grandfather...I...I just felt I had to do something about it. Take it. I want you to have it." I extended my hand, trying to hand her the money.

Her hand didn't meet mine. Sophie didn't move and just looked at me, not saying a thing. I could see she was thinking, trying to determine what to do or say next.

"Put the money back in your pocket, Leo," she said calmly.

I was confused. "Why? You know you need the money, Sophie. Take it." I extended my hand even farther toward her. Sophie didn't move and just kept staring at me.

"Look, thanks for thinking of me and wanting to help, but I'm fine. Really. I'll ask if I need it, OK?"

"But we both know you need it. You're just being proud and stubborn." I raised my voice.

Sophie looked at me with her ever-deep black eyes. "Yeah. You're right. I am proud," she said quietly, almost whispering. She turned and started walking away.

"Suit yourself," I said as I looked at Sophie getting farther away on the long stretch of pavement that led to the school entrance.

I felt angry. I shoved the bills back into my pocket and swore not to talk to her ever again—a promise I knew I couldn't keep.

We didn't speak a word for the rest of that day, and we didn't even walk together back home.

During the next several days, we didn't meet or speak to each other. My afternoons suddenly became empty, and the only good thing about it was that I made good progress with my comic book.

I now had all the characters I needed to build the story that had been swirling in my mind for a while. It was about a family of super-heroes, all of them able to transform between good and evil forms of themselves. I had the storyline all figured out and just needed the time to draw it.

As I came out of my house one afternoon, I saw Sophie raking our neighbor's lawn on the other side of the street.

I stood on the road, looking at her. She noticed me and stopped raking. Sophie looked sweaty, dirty, and full of energy—all at the same time.

I tried to remind myself I was angry with her, but it didn't help. I found myself walking toward her as if she was a magnet. I had to talk to her.

"What's this?" I pointed at the rake.

"Work. It pays pretty well. I put flyers in people's mailboxes, and it works," Sophie replied, leaning on the rake's handle.

I looked at the grass behind her and saw the lines the rake made. They were perfectly straight as if someone had painted stripes of different shades of green on that lawn.

"That's cool. Looks kind of hard," I said calmly, trying not to show any excitement so maybe she would notice I was still mad at her.

"Are you offering me help again?" Sophie asked flatly.

I felt my face slowly turning red. "No...I just..." I started muttering, but then I saw Sophie's lips move, then twitch, turning into a big smile that spread all over her face.

We looked at each other for a moment, and in perfect synchronization, we burst out laughing.

"Hey, seriously." Sophie wiped her forehead with the back of her hand. "I could use some help, and I think we will be able to make much more money if we work together. What do you say?" She pointed at the rake.

"Hmm." I crossed my arms over my chest and started thinking about what it would mean to work in the afternoons with her.

"Come on, Leo. We'll make good money. You'll even be able to save for that Rocket skateboard you want so much," she said, grinning.

Sophie made a good point. I really wanted that skateboard. I knew it'd be hard work, but it also meant spending more time with Sophie again.

"You need that money for the immigration lawyer, don't you?" I asked.

"I do," she admitted. "It's important."

"OK," I said and reached out to shake her hand. "You have a partner."

And so we started raking leaves, weeding, and cleaning backyards for hours every week. Sophie would go from door to door, handing out handwritten flyers about our gardening service. People liked the idea of neighborhood kids starting a business initiative, and soon our afternoons and weekends were fully booked.

The first week was kind of painful. I had stinging blisters on my hands from the rake's wooden handle. Sophie had blisters as well but never complained. Instead, she bought us each a pair of gloves. We also used some of the money we'd made to get a wheelbarrow and several tools to help us work faster.

We worked hard and got more efficient every day. We split the work between us—I would rake the lawns, and Sophie would pile everything up into large brown paper bags. Then we'd carry them together to the dumpster. I would take short breaks, but Sophie would stop only to get a drink of water.

One time, when I asked her why she seemed always to be in a hurry, she said, "There's a book next to my bed waiting for me."

CHAPTER 6

RELIGION OF REASON

When my mother heard about our gardening work, she insisted I invite Sophie and her mother over for dinner on Friday night.

"You are spending so much time with that girl, and we don't know a thing about her," she said, and she made sure to remind me every day that week to invite Sophie.

It took me three days to finally bring it up with Sophie, and when I asked her as we came out of social studies class, she smiled and said, "Yes, tell your mother that I'll be there on Friday."

I noticed Sophie said "I" and not "we" but decided not to ask about it.

That Friday afternoon, I felt nervous about Sophie meeting my parents. At six thirty sharp, Sophie rang the doorbell.

My mother opened the door and greeted her with a big smile.

Sophie looked nice. She wore a dress I hadn't seen before—it looked new. It made me happy to think she could probably afford it because of the money we'd earned together. Her hair was braided in two perfectly symmetrical braids, which made it possible to see Sophie's face in a way I hadn't before.

"Oh my, look at you. It is so nice to meet you finally. You look gorgeous, Sophie. And look at those cute braids." My mother smiled as she closed the door behind her. My father turned around in his couch in the living room, looked at Sophie for a moment, and then turned back to his baseball game.

"I brought these." Sophie handed my mother a plate wrapped in a piece of aluminum foil. "Those are sweet pastries for dessert. They're called baklava. They're made from phyllo dough, walnuts, and some honey."

"Thank you, Sophie. Walnuts and honey? Oh, now I *have* to try one." My mother took the plate and led us toward the kitchen. Then she laid the plate on the countertop, unwrapped the foil, and took a bite from one of the pieces.

"My god, this is so good!" My mother looked genuinely surprised at how those strange-looking sweets tasted. I was happy to see her in such a good mood.

"I'm sorry my mother couldn't come; she's not feeling well lately," Sophie said, looking up at my mother.

"Oh, I'm sorry to hear that. I hope she feels better soon," my mother replied. She put her hand on Sophie's shoulder.

"Let's go eat dinner before I finish all these." My mother led us to the dining room and called my father to the table. As my father sat in the chair at the head of the table, he gave Sophie a little nod and then turned to scan the food on the table. That nod didn't seem like much, but I knew it meant he liked her.

"Paul, dear," my mother said as she sat down, "would you mind saying grace?"

We all lowered our heads and clasped our hands as my father led the prayer. I peeked to see that Sophie didn't put her hands together and didn't close her eyes. She just sat there and looked at me with a hint of a smile and with her eyes open.

When the time came to say "Amen," Sophie kept quiet. My mother gave her a look. I could almost read her mind: *What kind of person doesn't say 'Amen' after grace?*

Luckily Sophie didn't notice my mother, as she was looking at me.

My mother had made roasted chicken and mashed potatoes for dinner. We passed her our plates, and she served it to us. We waited for her to sit down and then started eating.

My mother asked about our gardening, and both Sophie and I described how we went around the neighborhood handing out handwritten brochures and how more and more people hired us to take care of their yards, lawns, and gardens.

He didn't say a word, but I could see it made my father happy.

As I passed the salad bowl to my father, my mother turned to Sophie and asked, "So what is your religion? Leo tells me you come from the Middle East. Are you Muslim?"

Sophie turned to look at me. I suddenly thought I might have made a mistake telling my mother that Sophie came from Syria. But at least I'd made sure not to say anything about her immigration problem.

"No, I'm not Muslim, Mrs. Weckl." Sophie smiled politely and turned back to look at her plate. I felt a little better.

"Oh, OK," my mother said and picked up the gravy boat. "Would you like some gravy on your potatoes, dear?" my mother asked Sophie, holding the gravy boat over her plate.

"No, thank you; I'm fine," Sophie said, waving her hand gently. My mother passed the gravy to my father, who kept quiet as usual.

My mother still seemed uneasy. She moved in her chair, and after a minute or so, she turned to Sophie again and asked, "So are you Christian...Jewish?"

I realized I had never talked about religion with Sophie before. I hadn't told her about my mother and how religious she was. Maybe I should have warned her about that before she came over.

My mother had a Bible on her nightstand and read it every night. Once, when I asked her about it, she told me that as soon as she would finish it, she'd immediately start all over again. I never understood how someone could read the same thing over and over. She also had a necklace with a cross on it and kissed it about fifty times a day.

She categorized people by their religion. For example, she referred to the family who lived next door as the "Hindu family" and called Laura, her best friend, "my dear Jewish friend."

Sophie continued to look down at her plate, and it took her a moment to look back at my mother. "I'm neither, Mrs. Weckl," she replied with a gentle smile. I felt Sophie was trying her best to be polite.

After we finished clearing the table, we sat in the living room, drank tea and ate Sophie's delicious baklavas. My mother really liked them. Just as I thought the evening would end well, my mother had to get back to religion. It was her sensitive spot, and I guess she couldn't help herself.

"I'm sorry I'm pressing on this point dear, but if you're not Christian, Jewish or Muslim—what are you?" she asked.

Sophie didn't reply immediately. She took a couple of long seconds and then said, "I'm just me, Mrs. Weckl. I am not religious."

"Oh, I see." My mother nodded. "So you don't practice any faith?"

"No, I try to practice reason," Sophie replied.

"Reason is great for some things in life, but you can't mix it with faith. Everyone has a right to their own views, though. I'm sorry if my questions made you feel uncomfortable," my mother said, smiling at Sophie, then taking another sip of her tea.

"It's OK," Sophie smiled back.

Although it seemed like the matter was resolved, there was still tension in the air. Everyone was quiet, and the longer that silence lingered, the more awkward it became. I was relieved when Sophie finally stood up, thanked everyone, and said she had to get going.

"So I will see you tomorrow morning at seven." Sophie turned to me as I walked her to the door.

"Yes, I'll come over to help with the wheelbarrow. Hey…" I whispered as I closed the door behind me. "I'm sorry about—"

"Don't worry about it," Sophie shook her head slightly.

We stood out on the wooden porch. Sophie looked beautiful with those braids and her blue dress.

"My mother sewed it for me," Sophie said, noticing I was looking at it. "And you really have nothing to be sorry about." She smiled. Sophie turned and walked away, disappearing into the darkness of the tree-covered trail that led to the park. I stood there on the porch for several minutes.

I wonder if she'll ever come back to my house again, I thought as I closed the door behind me.

CHAPTER 7

A BLUE KANGAROO

Sophie and I met early the next morning to work on Mr. Friedman's backyard, which was at the edge of our neighborhood. Mr. Friedman, the old man who taught Sophie's computer class, had a big lawn in the back of his one-story ranch house.

He had curly white hair, wore worn-out jeans and untucked buttoned shirts with Hawaiian prints, and always had a pair of sandals on his feet.

That Saturday, while we were working in his backyard, he came out and stood on the back porch, looking at us working. The sun was high in the sky, and both Sophie and I were working on the side of the yard that had no shade. Sophie was watering the soil around a group of boxwood shrubs, and I was on my knees, pulling weeds at the edge of the grass line.

"Are you drinking enough?" Mr. Friedman asked loudly with his arms crossed. "It's hot today, and I don't have insurance for dehydrated kids, you know..."

"I drank so much I could water your shrubs myself," I shouted back.

"Ha!" Mr. Friedman chuckled. "Well, I surely admire your diligence, kids. Good work." He turned and went back into the house through the sliding-glass door. Sophie stood and wiped the sweat from her forehead with the back of her hand.

"I like this guy," she said. She went to the wheelbarrow to get a spading fork. Sophie stuck the fork into the wet soil around the shrubs that surrounded the back of the house.

"Oh, wow! Look at that," she suddenly cried.

I walked toward her as she squatted, looking at an open ant colony the spading fork had just turned up from the ground. Ants ran all around, but Sophie just kept staring at the exposed nest.

"Look at this. It's so complex. It is like there is a mastermind behind all those ants working together. That is an egg chamber, and look at the larvae there." Sophie pointed at the part of the nest with what looked like little white dots.

"I hate ants," I said. I turned back to pulling weeds near the fence.

Sophie looked at those ants for another long minute and then started to turn the soil around the shrubs again. "So did your mother say anything about last night?" she asked.

"No, I didn't talk to her about it. But I could tell she wasn't happy. I should've warned you about how religious she is."

"It wouldn't have mattered; I would still have answered her questions the same way I did." Sophie lifted and turned over the wet soil.

"So what's that thing about not being religious?" I asked, still kneeling a few feet from her.

Sophie continued to push her spading fork into the ground, trying to take out the roots of an old, dry shrub. After a minute or so, she finally said, "I don't see a reason to believe in anything unless it is proven by facts and by science." Sophie looked at me for a quick second and then continued to wrestle the shrub's roots out of the ground.

"What does this have to do with science?" I retorted. Sophie stopped her work, stuck the spading fork in the ground, and turned to face me.

"I want to ask you something," Sophie said in a low voice as she walked closer, standing right above me.

"Shoot," I said, looking up.

"Can we agree that if we talk about those kinds of things, we do it so we can both learn from it, rather than argue? I don't want to argue; it doesn't lead anywhere. You saw how your mother reacted." Sophie gave me a questioning look.

"OK, I get it. Let's not argue, but can you answer my question? What does religion have to do with science?"

Sophie stood up, walked to the wheelbarrow, picked up two bottles of water, and walked back to where I was kneeling. She tossed one bottle toward me, and I grabbed it just as she sat down next to me.

"Look, it's easier if you forget, just for a second, everything that you were taught and take for granted. Think about things from scratch." Sophie took a sip from her bottle.

"OK." I nodded. "I'll try."

"So let me ask you a different question first: What is 'truth'? How do you know if something is true or not?" Sophie gazed at me, leaning on her knees with her elbows, waiting for me to respond.

"I don't know...I guess you need...proof," I said, thinking I should have a better answer to such a simple question.

"Right, and how do you prove something to be true?" Sophie took another sip and turned the cap on her water bottle slowly.

"With evidence," I said, and Sophie nodded, swallowing the sip of water in her mouth.

"So, in order to prove something, you have to have evidence and see it in reality or have a real and logical explanation for it. It's *reality* that tells us if something is there or not and if something happened or not."

I nodded. What Sophie was saying made sense to me.

Sophie smiled, laid her water bottle on the ground, and clasped her hands.

"My grandfather used to talk to me about those kinds of things. He told me that in court, for instance, if you want to prove that a suspect committed a crime, you need to prove it beyond a 'reasonable doubt.' So we rely on reason when it matters and when we really want to know the truth, because before we send someone to jail, we need to be pretty sure that they've committed the crime, right?"

"Yep." I nodded.

"So proof is about reason and science, not faith. It's about fingerprints on a gun, the suspect's hair at the scene of the crime, a motive—things like that. Real things. But when it comes to religion, people expect you to believe without proof."

Sophie looked at me for a long moment. She was leaning toward me as if to see how I would react to what she was saying. She was the first person to talk to me about religion this way, and I felt an urge to argue and defend everything I'd learned in Sunday school over the years.

"What if God is beyond reality, beyond science? What if you can't prove God?" I asked, genuinely curious about her answer to that question.

"Hmm..." Sophie hummed and looked down to the ground. She paused for a couple of seconds and then replied, still looking down, "That's an interesting question, but I think that there is a problem with the definition of reality here. If something exists, it has to be part of reality—that is the definition of reality, right? Reality is everything that exists. So nothing can be outside of it and still exist. And if it is part of reality, it should be proved."

"I get it, but you cannot prove that God *doesn't* exist." I shook my head.

Sophie closed her eyes and smiled.

"What? What are you smiling about?" I smiled back.

"Can you prove that there isn't a blue kangaroo jumping on your head right now?" Sophie pointed at an imaginary kangaroo over my head.

I gave Sophie a curious look. "What do you mean? You know there's nothing jumping on my head."

"And how about a red dragon or a white unicorn?"

"Come on, Soph. What are you trying to say?"

"I'm saying that, in science, you prove things to be true—not false. It is as if you put all the suspects of a crime in prison and ask them to prove they are innocent in order to be released. It's wrong. If you claim something to be true, *you* should prove it." Sophie raised herself and wiped the dirt off her hands. "We need to get back to work. We can talk more about this later," she said.

I nodded, and she turned back to her spading fork. I noticed my left shoelace had come untied, so I used the time to think a little about what Sophie had just said. I felt uncomfortable for some reason. Her words made sense, but they were the opposite of things I'd learned and believed to be true.

I got up, walked a couple of steps toward the garden's high wooden fence, and crouched down. The soil between the grass and the fence was filled with weeds. Sophie finished uprooting the dead shrub and placed it in the wheelbarrow. Then she came over and helped me with weeding the line of soil at the edge of the garden.

"Are you OK?" Sophie asked, looking at me at eye level as we both crouched.

"Yes, why?" I answered, my chin resting on my bent knees.

"I don't know. You look troubled."

"I'm just thinking about what you said." I raised my head to look at her. I noticed a line of brown dirt on her left cheek, so I touched my cheek to show her where it was. Sophie cleaned it off with her sleeve.

"So if you don't believe in God or religion, who do you think created the universe?" I asked.

"I don't think it was created. It's just like Mr. Sumner said: matter doesn't get created; it just changes form. But regardless, this is why physicists are researching space and trying to find explanations with theories like the Big Bang."

"You know, I've always thought 'Big Bang' sounds like a name for a movie rather than an explanation of how the world started," I joked.

We both giggled, and suddenly a dog started barking and making scratching noises on the other side of the fence. We were both startled and got up on our feet. The first time we'd come to work in Mr. Friedman's backyard, the same dog had barked for almost an hour until it got used to the idea we were working there.

"How about we call it a day?" Sophie suggested. "It's too hot today."

"Let's just finish this corner and go home," I said. I pointed at the back corner of the yard.

For the next five minutes, until we finished working, I was still having a discussion with Sophie in my head, playing both sides: Can I really question

God? And if there is no God, who decides what's right and what's wrong? I didn't have answers, but I found that I enjoyed trying to figure things out in my head, just by talking to myself.

We put all our tools in the wheelbarrow, and Sophie rang Mr. Friedman's doorbell. We heard a thump of something falling on the floor and then footsteps coming closer. Mr. Friedman opened the door, looking distracted. He was holding something that looked like a green board with many black rectangular pieces on it.

"Oh, I need to pay you—right." He smacked his forehead and then reached into his pocket, took out some dollar bills, and handed them to us. He was not counting them. Sophie was not looking at him, so I had to reach out and take the bills.

"This is too much," I said. I handed Mr. Friedman the extra amount.

"Just keep it. You guys are doing a great job back there," he said, looking at Sophie.

Sophie was fixated on the green board in his other hand. "What is that?" she asked.

"It's a computer motherboard. I mentioned it in the first lesson," Mr. Friedman replied. He handed it to Sophie.

"You didn't. You said you're going to talk about hardware components later in the course." Sophie took the board and examined it like it was a thing of wonder.

"Maybe you're right. I'm getting too old." Mr. Friedman smiled and leaned on the doorframe. "You know, I'm so old that I was part of the team that built one of the first personal computers back in the day."

"This is awesome." Sophie looked up at him. "I'm having so much fun learning how to program. I've built three programs already. The one you gave us for homework was pretty simple, so I came up with two more sorting programs."

"That's super, Sophia." Mr. Friedman looked pleased, and I realized he was the first person I'd heard call her Sophia.

"Here, I'll give you a couple of more advanced programming books." Mr. Friedman went back into the house and came back with two thick books. He handed them to Sophie, who looked thrilled and excited.

"Thank you so much, Mr. Friedman. I promise I will make good use of these." Sophie's eyes gleamed with excitement.

"I'm sure you will." Mr. Friedman smiled. "But *this* you don't get to keep." He pointed at the motherboard Sophie was still holding.

"Oh, sorry." She giggled and handed it back to Mr. Friedman.

We strolled back to Sophie's house. We were both exhausted from the long hours of work in the sun, but Sophie had this little smile on her face that made me feel good too.

We got to the small tin storage shed in Sophie's fenced yard. It was old and had many dents, but it kept our tools safe. After we put all the tools back in their places, Sophie closed the shed's door and turned to walk back to her house.

Sophie suddenly turned around, came closer to me, and hugged me. She wrapped her arms around me and squeezed me tight.

This time I hugged her back. I felt the warmth of her head against my chest and wondered if she could feel my heart, which suddenly had started pounding harder and faster.

Then she let go and stepped back.

"I like you, Leo Weckl," she said, trying to curb her smile. I smiled back at her, and we looked straight at each other for a brief moment. My heart was still pounding, and I wanted to say something but couldn't find the words.

"Now get out of here." She pushed me gently by the shoulder.

Sophie picked up the books, which had been lying at the bottom of her porch's stairs. She turned to look at me, smiled, and then turned back toward the front door. When she opened the door, I could see her mother sitting in their living room, and I could hear her coughing before the door closed behind Sophie.

❖ ❖ ❖

When I got home, many cars filled our driveway. When I opened the door, loud chatting and laughing filled the living room. There were about fifty women in our house, and I recognized most of them from our church. A red-and-white-striped poster on the wall proclaimed, "Ingrid Sanders for Mayor."

It was easy to spot Ingrid in the small crowd; she was taller than most women and wore a bright-yellow suit. My mother was next to her, talking to Ingrid and another woman I didn't know.

A table next to the right wall of the living room held plates of biscuits and cookies and pitchers of lemonade.

I could use one of those cookies, I thought as I walked toward the staircase up to my room.

As I went up the staircase, I noticed that my mother, Mrs. Sanders, and the other woman were all looking at me. I could tell they were talking about me, and I even picked up on my mother whispering the word "Sophie" to Ingrid. Ingrid looked straight at me with a calm face and a hint of a smile as I went toward my room.

My father came out of the bathroom in the middle of the hall leading to the bedrooms. He was holding a newspaper under his arm and started walking toward my parents' bedroom.

"What's all this downstairs?" I asked him.

My father turned slowly with a weary face. "Your mother wants to be a politician now." He turned back to enter his bedroom.

"What do you mean?"

"She's getting involved in Ingrid's campaign. Pfft." My father grumbled, waved his hand, and then closed the bedroom door behind him. I went into my room and closed my door as well.

I lay on my bed and thought about my discussion with Sophie and how my mother would have reacted if she'd overheard it.

My mother was announcing something downstairs, and then Ingrid Sanders started to talk. I opened my door slightly to hear what she was saying.

"These elections are more important than ever before. We're in a do-or-die situation for our way of living and our social values. If we work together and win, we will bring equality and fairness back to this city. We will build better schools, provide housing and health care for the poor, and bring back a sense of community and social responsibility. Joe Triolesta and his selfish capitalist friends should go home!" she announced, and everyone cheered and clapped.

I closed my door and plopped down into the chair next to my desk.

It's weird, I thought. I couldn't decide if Ingrid Sanders was a good or a bad person. She seemed to want to do good things, but something about what she'd said just didn't seem right.

I grabbed my sketch pad from the back of my closet. I was tired from the hours of gardening, but I had an idea for a new character that I didn't want to lose.

Later that evening, at the dinner table, my mother and father argued as I'd never heard them before. My father usually avoided lengthy discussions, but this time he got angry and raised his voice, which he seldom did.

"I care about this, Paul! We need to stop the rich from getting richer and make sure the poor get what they deserve!" my mother replied after my father said he didn't understand why she was getting so involved with Ingrid's campaign.

"Deserve? People *deserve* what they *earn*! Rich people earn their money, unless they are corrupted by politicians like Ingrid Sanders!" My father's face turned red with anger.

"Ingrid Sanders will get elected; you can be sure about that!" My mother pointed at my father. "She is the only one brave enough to tax the rich and give more to the people who need it."

"And then we will all be poor!" he said and then went upstairs in the middle of dinner.

"I don't understand how he can defend those capitalist pigs." My mother got up angrily and went to the kitchen. She picked up the phone that hung on the wall and called her friend Laura.

I helped clean up the table, and as I was getting things back to the kitchen, I overheard my mother complaining to Laura about my father. As I was putting things back in the refrigerator, I heard my mother quietly say, "Do you promise not to tell anyone?"

I got a little closer and heard her whisper, "I am taking notes in Triolesta's meetings. I copy them and give them to Ingrid's assistant."

She paused for a quick second.

"I know. It's all for a good purpose," she continued.

I closed the refrigerator door and went back to the dinner table. I wasn't sure if my mother realized I'd overheard what she said.

Wow, my mother is spying for Ingrid Sanders, I thought.

I went up to my room and sat back down to add more detail to the new character I'd started drawing before dinner. As I moved my pencil back and forth, shading my character's clothes, I suddenly noticed I was smiling.

I was thinking of how Sophie had said, "I like you, Leo Weckl."

CHAPTER 8

GASPING FOR AIR

Days went by, and Sophie and I worked hard and saved more money. I bought the wide-wheel skateboard I wanted so badly and was riding it every spare moment I had. Sophie, on the other hand, didn't buy anything for herself—she just saved as much as she could for the immigration lawyer.

She was buying groceries every other day after school and also passed through the pharmacy to buy medicine. Her mother's coughing got worse and worse, and Sophie spent most of what she earned on her mother's pills.

Whenever we came back from work to put our tools in the little tin shed, I could hear Mrs. Anwar's hacking cough getting louder and more frequent.

One early Friday afternoon, Sophie waited for me outside with the wheelbarrow and two rakes in it. We were going to cut the grass in Mr. Friedman's yard using his loud lawnmower.

"What's with the serious face?" I asked Sophie as we walked along the side of the road. She was looking down, staring at the pavement. Her mind was somewhere else.

"My grandfather's friend from back in Syria wired us fifteen hundred dollars. He said that my grandfather left that money with him and told him that he wanted me to have it. He also said that the Syrian government confiscated my grandparents' house and everything in it. They took everything because now my father owns it, and he is still in jail accused of treason."

"Wow." I looked at her with wonder. This whole story felt like it came out of a movie script or something.

"Yes. I thought about it a lot. Fifteen hundred dollars is a lot of money, and my mom and I could surely use some of it." Sophie exhaled heavily. "But I've decided that our immigration status is the most important thing, so I'm going to give it to the lawyer tomorrow."

"If you give that money to the lawyer, that means you almost have all the money for the immigration process, right?" I tried to cheer her up.

"Almost. I managed to save just a little over three hundred, so I'll be about two hundred short of the five grand. In two or three weeks, I can save the rest and start the immigration status change process," Sophie said, still not showing any signs of joy or enthusiasm.

"So you're getting close, Soph! It'll be fine, you'll see. Just a couple of weeks more, and you and your mother will be safe."

"That's the problem. For some weird reason, I feel like our time is running out. I keep thinking about being sent back to Syria..." Sophie pursed her lips. She looked worried in a way I'd never seen before.

I was trying to imagine what it would mean for her to go back to her homeland, with her grandfather gone, her father charged with treason and kept in some forsaken jail, and her mother sick.

"I won't let that happen, Soph; I promise." I got close to her and put my hand on her shoulder. Sophie stopped, lowered the wheelbarrow, and stood for a second. I stopped as well.

She turned and smiled at me. "Thanks, Leo. You're the best best friend anyone could ever have." I smiled back, feeling my face turning a little red as we kept walking toward Mr. Freidman's house.

An hour or so later, when we were taking a break from mowing the grass on Mr. Friedman's front lawn, Sophie took something that looked like a catalog out from her pocket. She turned away to hide it from me, so I did the only logical thing—I grabbed it out of her hand and started running, trying to read it as I did. All I could see were pictures of big telescopes and their prices.

"Hey, come back here!" Sophie shouted and started chasing me. I circled the house and ended up right in front of the cut-grass pile. I jumped right into it and threw a handful of cut grass at Sophie, who was getting ready to dive in as well. Sophie dove in, and suddenly, I felt her hands touching my belly, tickling me. We rolled together, grass getting into our hair, clothes, and mouths.

"Stop, stop, I surrender!" I shrieked after a couple of seconds.

Tickling wasn't something I could handle, so I gave up, throwing the catalog up in the air. We were both laughing and ended up lying on our backs, brushing the grass off our faces and spitting it out of our mouths.

"Anything but tickling," I panted, and Sophie giggled. We lay on the grass, looking up at the blue sky above us.

"Telescopes?" I turned to Sophie as I crossed my arms under my head.

"Yes, I found this website, and I ordered their catalog. It arrived today." Sophie swiped her hand across her forehead to remove another piece of grass.

"Planning to buy one?"

"No, you know I can't afford it." Sophie rolled slightly toward me. Her face was calm and relaxed.

"Isn't it amazing to think that we're lying here on a ball that is floating in space?" she asked. She rolled back and looked up at the blue sky above us. "And this fireball sending us rays of energy that makes all this possible?" She raised the hand holding the catalog upward. "And to think that there are billions and billions of planets and stars out there..."

"I try not to think about it—it makes me…nervous," I whispered.

"I think it is so…fascinating," Sophie whispered back, and then suddenly, Mr. Friedman appeared right in front of us.

We hadn't heard him getting close, and we were both startled. We got up on our feet quickly. Mr. Friedman wore ridiculously large sunglasses and a hat with a wide brim and a long strap that dangled under his chin.

"It's a beautiful day, isn't it?" he said, smiling.

"Yes, it is," Sophie replied, brushing grass off her shirt. All of a sudden, the catalog she was holding fell out of her hand and rolled toward Mr. Friedman's feet.

"What's this?" he asked, picking it up.

"It's nothing—just a telescope catalog I was looking through." Sophie shrugged.

"Hmm, interested in astronomy?" Mr. Friedman handed her back the catalog.

"I am." Sophie nodded.

"Good." He nodded back. "Take your time, kids; I'm going to go for a short walk. Here is your pay for the day." He took money out of his shirt pocket, handed it to me, and turned to walk away.

"He's a little weird, don't you think?" I whispered, looking at Mr. Friedman strolling down the sidewalk, his hands behind his back.

"I like his type of weird," Sophie replied. "He's interesting and...original." We stood there for a couple of seconds, looking at Mr. Friedman as he shrank into the distance.

"OK, back to work." Sophie shoved the catalog back into her pocket, picked up the rake, and started raking the grass into a pile again.

Later that evening, as we were putting our tools back in the shed next to Sophie's house, the front door opened. Sophie's mother was standing at the door, wearing a long black gown. She had a white scarf tied around her shoulders, and she was barefoot. When she looked up at Sophie, I could see she was in terrible pain. Then she started coughing heavily, both her hands clutching at her chest.

Sophie dropped the rake she was holding and ran toward her mother. Just as Sophie got to the door, her mother fell to her knees, her hands moving up from her chest to the bottom of her throat. Sophie grabbed her and talked to her in Arabic.

"She can't breathe! She can't breathe!" Sophie cried. "Call an ambulance. Hurry!"

I started running toward the house but then heard Sophie shouting, "We don't have a phone, Leo. Run to your house! Quick!"

I turned and ran toward my house. I ran through the park as fast as I could and raced into the house toward the kitchen phone. Luckily, no one was there to ask questions. I picked up the phone and dialed 911.

I was breathing heavily while explaining to the woman on the phone how to get to the brown house next to the park, as I couldn't remember Sophie's exact address. The woman on the other end of the line assured me they were sending an ambulance right away.

I hung up and ran back outside toward the park. I ran as fast as I could and felt my lungs starting to burn as I got closer to Sophie's house. Sophie was leaning over her mother on the wooden porch, talking to her and stroking her hair gently. I opened the gate, ran up the porch stairs, and knelt next to Sophie. I saw that Sophie had taken off her mother's scarf and loosened the gown around her neck. She was caressing her mother's forehead, talking to her in Arabic.

"They said they're coming as fast as possible," I whispered. Sophie nodded, not taking her eyes off her mother. Her mother's breath made a wheezing sound, and it looked like it was extremely difficult for her to inhale. Sophie kept talking to her mother, moving her hands and breathing with her; from what I could gather, she was telling her to relax and breathe slowly through her nose.

We heard a siren in the distance getting louder.

A minute later, two paramedics jumped out of an ambulance, running toward us. They asked Sophie several questions, and then one of them went back to the ambulance and got a stretcher. They lifted Sophie's mother onto it and took her into the ambulance. Sophie climbed up to the back of the ambulance after them, just before they closed the door. Before I could do or say anything, the ambulance took off, its siren wailing. I watched the ambulance turn right out of our neighborhood toward the nearby hospital.

I walked back toward Sophie's house, closed the front door, and finished putting our tools in the shed. As I closed the gate behind me, I stood still for a minute, trying to think about what had just happened.

The sun was setting slowly behind the park's trees, coloring the clouds in a bright pinkish glow. I slid my hands into my pockets and walked back home. When I got there, my mother and father were sitting in the living room, speaking calmly for a change. I went right up to my room. I didn't feel like talking to anyone.

❖ ❖ ❖

The next morning, I went straight to Sophie's house. I knocked on the door, but no one answered. I took a couple of steps back to look at the windows but saw no movement inside the house.

As I closed the gate behind me, I saw Sophie walking on the sidewalk toward me, holding grocery bags, one in each hand. She looked tired, but I could see she was happy to see me.

As she got closer to me, she lowered the bags to the ground, walked up to me, put her arms around me, and hugged me tightly. I hugged her back.

Sophie kept hugging me and didn't let go. We stood there for a long minute, not saying a word, just hugging each other. Her hands were locked around my waist, and my hands were wrapped around her shoulders.

I could feel Sophie's breath, and I could smell the scent of her hair. Her cheek was pressed against my chest, moving up and down with my own breath.

I felt Sophie didn't want to talk, so I just kept hugging her.

I heard Sophie sniffling gently, and she lifted her head, looking up at me.

"It turns out she has a lung disease that requires special treatment. She has an oxygen tank now, and she feels better than before. By the time we got to the hospital, she could hardly breathe, and the doctor said that if we hadn't gotten there in time, she could have suffocated. Thanks for calling the ambulance so quickly," she said with a grateful look.

Sophie looked down to the bags lying on the sidewalk but didn't pick them up.

"What's wrong?" I asked, bending my knees a little so I could see her face.

"I won't be able to continue our work in gardening," Sophie replied. "I made some calculations and decided to take another job that pays better. I have to make more money, Leo. The hospital visit was so expensive that I have no money left to give to the lawyer. The fifteen hundred that my grandfather left us and the money I saved—it's almost all gone. I'm back to being two thousand dollars short. I even called the lawyer to ask him for some of the money back, but he wouldn't give it to me. He said he already used it. If I only knew this would happen...I..." Sophie raised her head and looked at me. Her face was tender and soft, and I felt helpless, not knowing how to help her.

"Do you need some money, Soph? I saved some. I'll give it to you."

"Thanks, Leo, but it'll be fine. I'm starting to work in cleaning, and I'll make some good money soon." Sophie lowered her head and looked away.

"Where are you going to work?" I asked.

"It doesn't matter. They are taking a risk by letting a thirteen-year-old girl work for them, so I'd rather people not know." Sophie picked up the bags, stood next to me for a brief second, and then walked through the gate and into her house.

I stood there for a couple of minutes, looking at Sophie's closed door. Several thoughts were going through my head, but the one that bothered me most of all was that I wanted Sophie to need me more, to want my help.

I could see how it made sense for her to go work in a job that made more money, but after all, we would lose what we'd built, and we wouldn't get to spend time together.

I stayed in my room all that evening, drawing. I broke the tip of my pencil over and over and realized I was still feeling frustrated, disappointed, and even a little angry with Sophie. Gardening was hard, but we had fun working and making money together—I didn't want it to end.

The following week, we walked together around the neighborhood, telling our customers that we would not be continuing our work. When we got to Mr. Friedman, he just said, "Oh, no, no, out of the question—you're not going to make me find another gardener. I'll double your pay if you stay."

Sophie turned to me and asked, "Can you work here on Sunday mornings? That's the only time I have."

"No, I can't. I have to go to church with my parents on Sundays," I reminded her.

Sophie thought for a brief second and told Mr. Friedman, "I will work your garden Sunday mornings by myself, if that's OK with you."

"Deal," Mr. Friedman said. He closed the door behind him.

We continued our tour without saying a word to each other.

❖   ❖   ❖

Spring break came along, and now that I wasn't working as I used to, I felt a void. I started meeting with my bike buddies again. We took long rides into the fields, trying to find deserted farmhouses and other hiding spots. We found an empty old factory that had big windows on its back wall, which was two stories high. We spent the afternoon throwing stones at them, enjoying the sound of the breaking glass.

We called ourselves "Black Raiders" and made up songs with curse words. But after a while, I realized I didn't enjoy it as much as I used to. All the boys talked about were girls and video games, and they told dirty jokes that weren't even funny.

So I started spending more time in my room, drawing. I continued the story about the family of superheroes. They all had different super-powers, and each had two forms—one good and one evil. They would transform from one form to another, scheming and fighting about how to either destroy or save the world, depending on their form—just like Dr. Jekyll and Mr. Hyde but with galactic superpowers.

After a couple of days of spending all my time locked in my room, making my mother worried that I was becoming "antisocial," I finished it.

The following Sunday, right after we came back from another dull morning at my mother's church, I rode my bike to Mr. Friedman's house. I had to show my story to Sophie. As I expected, Sophie was there, working in the backyard.

Sophie was happy to see me.

"I need a break," she declared, and we sat down on the back lawn. Sophie suddenly stood up. "I need my water bottle." She went back to the wheelbarrow.

When I looked back at Sophie, I noticed a pile of thick books piled next to Mr. Friedman's sliding door that led to the backyard. I turned my head sideways to read the title on the spine of one of the books—it said *Object-Oriented Programming*.

When Sophie returned, she put her hand on my back, up between my shoulder blades, just below my neck. She sat next to me holding her water bottle.

I looked at her, and I realized how much I had missed being with her.

"What have you been up to?" she asked after sipping some water.

I took the finished comic book out of my bag and handed it over to her. She smiled and started reading it eagerly. She dove into the book, reading quickly and turning the pages one after another.

"This is awesome!" she said as she turned the last page over. "The characters are so real and interesting. I love that the evil form of the mother ends up saving the good form of the father without intending to. And then the part where he destroys the evil forms altogether and saves the galaxy...

it's a smart plot, Leo." Sophie smiled a little smile, but it was one that made me feel enormously proud.

"Thanks," I murmured. I'd been anxious to hear what Sophie thought about my story and was relieved that she liked it.

"You have to print this. The drawings are amazing. Kids will love reading it." Sophie stood up.

"Print it?" I replied, standing up next to her. "Where would I print it? And who would buy it?" The thought of doing something with my story hadn't even crossed my mind.

"Let's meet tomorrow after school and do some research," Sophie said in an assertive tone. "I have to get back to work now, but printing it shouldn't cost too much, and I'm sure we can find a bookstore that'll sell it." Sophie went back to pruning Mr. Friedman's boxwood shrubs.

After printing twenty copies of the comic book in a nearby print shop, Sophie and I went to two bookstores within walking distance from our neighborhood. The first bookstore owner refused politely, but the older woman who owned the second one said she would be happy to pay me a dollar apiece if she managed to sell them for two. That sounded like a good deal to me, and we left all twenty copies with her.

We stopped to celebrate in the nearby ice cream parlor, but as usual, Sophie wouldn't get any and instead watched me eat my plain chocolate scoop.

I sold twelve copies, which meant I didn't make much money, but that one time I saw a sixth-grade kid reading my comic book at school during recess was worth the whole thing. I felt happy and proud—I, Leo Weckl, had written a story that people paid money to read.

CHAPTER 9

GALILEO GALILEI

S pring break was over, and we went back to school. It was a beautiful spring morning, and as we passed a row of flowers to the left of the sidewalk, Sophie stopped to look at a big yellow butterfly on one of them.

"What a beautiful tiger swallowtail," she said, examining the butterfly from up close. I was not surprised she knew the precise type of that butterfly. Sophie knew things. And when I say "knew," I mean she *really* understood and remembered many things.

When we were looking for gardening tools in a shop one day, she remembered the name and price of every product we considered to buy. When we got out of that store, I joked with her that she must have a sophisticated recording machine implanted inside her brain, logging everything.

"Sound like a good idea for another superhero, don't you think?" Sophie grinned.

"Is that the book Mr. Friedman gave you?" I asked her about the book she was carrying. I thought I had seen that book before in a pile at Mr. Friedman's house the other day.

"Yes, it's a book about Internet programming," Sophie replied, turning the book so I could see its front cover. "I'm learning how to build websites that anyone can access. This Internet thing is going to change the world. One day it'll have everything on it—even this book."

I couldn't imagine how people would read books on computers.

"I'm not working this afternoon, so I'm going to the library to work on a computer there. Want to join me?"

"Hmm...I don't know. I do want to check if the new Celestia issue is out...so I might. By the way, if it did come out, you'll have to come pull me out of the comic book section when you finish. The next chapter is the final one, and it's supposed to be twice as long."

I opened the door to the school's long hallway.

After school, we walked together to the library. Sophie turned to the computer area, and I walked up to the librarian and asked if the new issue of the comic book had arrived.

"It just did. It is actually right here," the librarian said. She took it out of a box at the edge of her desk.

"Yes! Yes! Thank you!" I got so excited that I hopped a little. That made the librarian smile. A minute later, I was in one of Orthea's adventures.

When I looked at my watch again, I noticed a full hour had passed. After reading the whole story twice and examining every one of David Brankow's drawings carefully, I returned the comic book to the librarian and went to look for Sophie.

Sophie was typing fast on a keyboard with the big book lying open beside it. She was looking at the screen with an expression of sheer concentration and focus. I took a chair and sat next to her.

"What is this?" I asked, pointing at the monitor.

"Mr. Friedman challenged me to build a website, so I'm working on one," she replied, still staring at the screen.

I looked at the book next to the keyboard. The title of the page read "HTML."

"They did a lousy job with this template; I can't use it. I'll have to write it from scratch." Sophie shook her head as she typed text I couldn't understand on the screen. We left the library ten minutes later.

We went back to the library several times that week. I read the Celestia stories from the beginning, and Sophie worked on the computer until she had to leave for her cleaning work.

I didn't ask her again about where she was working. I figured that if she didn't want to tell me, I shouldn't ask.

"Why are you spending so much time on that website?" I asked her when we walked together one late afternoon to return two books to Mr. Friedman.

"I'm learning so much. I'm glad Mr. Friedman gave me that challenge. It wasn't easy, but it's the best way to learn. If I get good at programming, it might be a way for me to make money faster. Many businesses need websites. Maybe it will be my next business," she said enthusiastically.

We knocked on Mr. Friedman's door, and he opened it, wearing gray pants, a green plaid shirt, and a pair of slippers. His hair was messy, and he seemed distracted, as if we had interrupted him.

Sophie handed the books back to him and said, "I'm almost done with the website, and I plan to publish it next week. I could have used some ready-made templates but decided to build it from scratch to get more practice."

Mr. Friedman smiled. He looked at her and nodded. "Good thinking, girl."

"This book about Alan Turing and Van Neumann Architecture is amazing," Sophie said, pointing to the book that was now in Mr. Friedman's hands. "And I also loved the object-oriented book—it's fascinating. I was thinking about whether we could program a computer to reflect not only objects as they are in reality, but also to have objects seek goals, like living things do. You know what I mean?"

I looked at Sophie. Her face was glowing with excitement.

Mr. Friedman's eyes opened wide, and I was worried for a moment. His expression looked like he was getting angry, but just as I thought of taking a step back, his face changed. His eyes squinted a little, and his mouth opened to a big smile that turned into a big laugh. Mr. Friedman laughed a hearty belly laugh.

When he stopped laughing, he turned to look at Sophie.

"Ah, this is incredible. Did you think about this idea yourself, kid?" Mr. Friedman asked in a soft tone I hadn't heard before. His face looked much younger suddenly. His cheeks turned a little red, and he seemed genuinely excited about Sophie's comment.

"Yes, I did. It seems like a natural progression from object-oriented programing, right?" Sophie replied, looking a bit amused herself.

"That's a very advanced thought. I think you have a bright future ahead of you, Sophia," he said. He opened the door a little wider. "Come in for a moment. I have something for you."

Sophie and I looked at each other. In all the months we had worked for Mr. Friedman, we'd never gotten to see the inside of his house. He always came outside when he wanted to talk to us or bring us something to drink.

The house was a little dark, some curtains were almost completely shut, and the air felt stuffy and muggy. An enormous library covered an entire wall of the living room.

Mr. Friedman turned to us and said, "Stay here for a second, I'll be right back." He walked into one of the rooms.

Sophie scanned the bookshelves from side to side, her hand hovering over the books' spines gently, her head slightly tilted to read the titles.

I looked around. From the back window, I could see the backyard we knew so well and the tall, brown fence that surrounded it. A big desk stood in an awkward place between the living room and the kitchen. On it were a desktop computer and green electrical boards with a soldering iron next to them.

Mr. Friedman came back holding a long box. He put it on the floor next to Sophie and exhaled. "Phew, this is a bit heavier than I remembered," he said. He started tapping his fingers on the top of the box, looking at Sophie. "I bought this years ago and used it only a couple of times. When you told me you're interested in astronomy, I remembered that this thing was collecting dust in my closet." Mr. Friedman smiled, and Sophie's eyes lit up.

"No way!" she cried. She took two steps back and put both her palms to her mouth.

"You can have it. You'll make much better use of it than I would. Take it—it's yours."

Sophie stood still for a couple of seconds, astonished. She looked at me and then back at Mr. Friedman. She then opened her arms, walked forward, and hugged Mr. Friedman around his waist.

Mr. Friedman looked down at Sophie, surprised. His hands spread to the sides. He was looking at me as if he was not sure of what to do next. A moment later he wrapped his hands around her head, hugging her back, smiling. I am not sure, but I think his eyes were tearing up a bit.

Sophie thanked Mr. Friedman fifty times before we left his house. Sophie let me carry the telescope all the way back home. She was gleaming with joy.

"I don't know if I'll be able to sleep tonight. I want to put it together and calibrate it," she said as we approached her house.

"So just do it. I sometimes draw till I drop dead. It's the best way to fall asleep."

We laid the telescope down on Sophie's porch.

"I have to wake up early tomorrow. I want to show the website I've built to Mr. Sumner. I decided to build a website for our school. It's a surprise. Will you come with me? I want to be there before first period." Sophie was trying to lift the telescope by herself to check if she could carry it inside on her own. She seemed able to handle it.

"Sure, I'll meet you by the tree at seven tomorrow. See you," I said. I turned to walk back to my house. I didn't get why Sophie liked this Mr. Sumner so much.

We met near our tree at seven the next morning.

On our way to school, we saw a truck full of signs of the type you stick in the ground with a metal bracket. They had "Sanders for Mayor" printed on them, with the same colors of the sign that had been hanging on the wall in my house the other day. A guy was jumping on and off the truck, sticking signs in the ground every fifty feet or so.

"Elections are next month. Ingrid is putting a lot of money into this campaign. She really wants to win this time. My mother is working for her campaign almost every afternoon, and my dad is furious about it." I shook my head as we passed the long row of signs. "Triolesta is going to have a real challenge getting reelected this time. A lot of people support Sanders."

"Yes, it seems like it." Sophie nodded.

When we got to school, we asked Ms. White to call Mr. Sumner from the teacher's lounge. Mr. Sumner was cheerful as always and was holding a coffee mug. He was wearing brown corduroy pants, an orange shirt, and a dark-gray tie that had a drawing of Albert Einstein with his tongue sticking out.

So cheesy, I thought.

"Hey, Sophie, hey, Leo—what are you guys doing here so early?" he asked. He took a sip of coffee.

"I wanted to show you something I've been working on for a while. It's a website. I can show it to you on one of the computers in the library," Sophie said in a shy tone I'd never heard before.

"Wow, that sounds super exciting, Sophie, but I have to get ready for our science class now. Can we do it during recess later today?" Mr. Sumner asked, raising his eyebrows.

"Sure, we'll be here." Sophie nodded. She was unusually polite when talking to Sumner, and I didn't like it one bit.

When Mr. Sumner entered the class, he carried a box full of balls and marbles of different sizes. Everyone became quiet and waited in anticipation for the science mystery.

"Ready for our mystery, detectives?" Mr. Sumner asked, rubbing his hands together.

"Yes!" everyone answered together.

"So here is Galileo Galilei standing on top of the Leaning Tower of Pisa, dropping two balls to the ground—one big and heavy and one small and rather light in mass. 'Which one will hit the ground first?' he thought. What do you think? Can you help Galileo figure it out?"

"The heavier one! The big one!" many kids shouted.

"At the same time," Daniel and Sophie said almost in perfect synchronization.

"What?" Manu turned to nerdy Daniel, who sat behind him. "No way!"

"OK, guys, let's find out for ourselves. Follow me!" Mr. Sumner picked up the box and walked us outside. He had Big Frankie stand on the top of a picnic table in the schoolyard and drop different balls down to the ground.

"Boom! I told you so!" I heard Daniel say to Manu as the balls hit the ground at the same exact time.

The next period got replaced with a state assessment test Mrs. Ripley said was "very important." It was a hard test, and when we were walking out of class, I heard several of my classmates complaining that they didn't understand many of the questions.

"It isn't fair to test on stuff we haven't learned yet," Chloe complained to Mrs. Ripley.

"I'm not the one designing those tests, dear," Mrs. Ripley grunted back at her.

It was recess time, and Sophie and I stood outside the teachers' lounge until Mr. Sumner came out to follow us to the library. Once there, Sophie showed him the finished website on the computer in the corner of the room.

It had our school's logo and paragraphs with underscored text that led to different pages when you clicked it. There was information about the school's vision, the staff, the teachers, and even the cafeteria menu.

Mr. Sumner clasped his hands together and laughed, his eyes opened with excitement and wonder.

"Wow, Sophie." He beamed. "When did you learn to program? That is so professional! Wait until Principal Palmer sees this; he won't stop talking about the fact that our school needs a website." Mr. Sumner leaned over to look closer at the monitor. "This is amazing. Thanks for showing me this, Sophie." He stood up and left the library, heading toward the school's front office.

❖ ❖ ❖

That Sunday night, Sophie and I walked out to an open field near the creek, where it was completely dark. Sophie set up the telescope on the tripod and aimed it at the full moon. She turned several knobs on it and took a long look into the eyepiece. A sigh came out of her mouth.

"Oh...wow...Leo." Sophie gasped. "Look at that. You've got to see this!"

She stood up and pointed at the eyepiece. Her eyes sparkled with excitement.

I put my eye against the telescope's eyepiece and saw the moon as if it was right in front of me. "Look at that! Did you see that huge crater at the bottom?"

"That's Tyco...isn't it beautiful? It has peaks right in the center of it." Her voice was trembling.

We stayed in that field for quite some time.

As we put the telescope back in its bag, I looked at my watch and realized it had gotten late. I knew I would have some explaining to do when I got back home, but it was worth it. It was worth it, because when I looked at Sophie walking back home next to me, the side of her face white in the moonlight, I saw the happiest face I have ever seen.

CHAPTER 10

ANTS AND SHARING

"Can you stop messing with those ants already? We are wasting all of our recess time." I threw my hands up in frustration.

Sophie was squatting, looking at an anthill again at the edge of our schoolyard. Her elbows were on her knees, and her chin was resting on the back of her arms.

"Those insects are just amazing. So efficient," Sophie said, totally ignoring my comment. I looked at her, trying to find something nasty to say—but I couldn't.

She is just doing her thing, I thought.

"Would you want to be an ant?" I asked. I squatted next to her holding a dry stick I'd found by the tree next to us.

"No, of course not. Look at them, walking in a line like programmed robots. I wish one of them would just leave and do its own thing—but they can't; it's not their nature." Sophie shook her head while still looking at the ant trail.

"Hey, Sophie." We heard a voice from behind us.

We turned around. I was wondering who would come all the way to the edge of the schoolyard to talk to us. Nancy Sanders was standing behind us. "I heard you got a new telescope." Nancy grinned.

Sophie stood up and faced Nancy. "Yes, I did," she replied. She looked at me as she did. I remembered mentioning Sophie's telescope to Chloe. I regretted it already.

"Good for you." Nancy smiled, looking around to try to figure out what exactly we were up to. She was holding her notebook close to her chest with her arms crossed over it. Her hips were slowly rocking from side to side, making her dress sway gently as well.

"I'm trying to arrange some activities for Opposite Day, and I thought it would be nice if you brought your telescope to class and gave the students a chance to see the stars. A great idea, don't you think?" Nancy smiled and looked at me as if she was expecting me to nod back in approval.

On Opposite Day, which had been a school tradition for many years, kids would come to school in the late afternoon in their pajamas and do all sorts of fun activities. Then we would go to sleep in our sleeping bags in our classroom.

Sophie thought for a couple of seconds. Her forehead showed her funny thinking wrinkles.

"My telescope is very sensitive and can easily break, so I don't think it's a good idea," she replied, looking back at Nancy.

The smile disappeared from Nancy's face. "Hmm..." she tilted her head and gazed at Sophie. She didn't seem to be surprised and started nodding in a way that looked like she had just realized something new. "I was wondering if I should even bother asking you—I guess I should've known better."

Nancy took a step back and turned to walk away. Suddenly, she turned again and faced Sophie, her eyes narrowed and her mouth curved downwards into a contemptuous look. "Every student has *the right* to learn about the stars, you know—even students who can't afford a telescope."

I wanted to tell Nancy Sophie had gotten the telescope as a gift, but Sophie was already talking.

"How come students have a *right* to use my telescope? Does the fact that I have a telescope create a right for them to use it? Do you know what the word *right* even means?" Sophie asserted.

"Ha!" Nancy chuckled and took a small step forward. "You're asking *me* if I know what a right is? *I am* the one who's trying to make sure students get what they deserve from selfish people like you," Nancy pointed at Sophie.

"You have it all backwards, don't you?" Sophie said in a low tone that reminded me of the way she talked to Manu when she faced him in the school's backyard. "If you took the time to *really* understand what a right is you'd learn that it is something that protects you. Something people *cannot* do to you, not something they owe you."

"Let me get this straight. You're saying that people don't have the right to... let's say, food?" Nancy raised her eyebrows in astonishment.

"They don't, because if they did, then you'd have to force someone to make food for them, and that would be a contradiction – wouldn't it?"

"That's ridiculous! You are just trying to justify the simple fact that you're selfish— that's all. I guess you've never heard about 'sharing is caring'—have you? I don't know where you come from, but I guess they didn't teach you that over there." Nancy didn't wait for a reply. She turned around and left hastily.

Sophie stood still, watching Nancy as she walked away.

"Don't mind her." I shook my head.

"I don't." Sophie picked up her plastic bag, and we walked back to the school building.

When we entered our classroom, most of the kids were whispering and looking at us. It was clear Nancy had already told everyone about her chat with Sophie. Sophie was calm and didn't seem to care about the looks several kids gave her as she walked between the rows of desks toward the back of the room.

"Keeping the stars to ourselves, are we, Selfish Sophie?" asked Big Frankie, who was sitting two rows in front of Sophie. Judging by the laughter, many kids found it to be quite hilarious.

Sophie stood up, her chair making a screeching sound as she pushed it back. She looked around the class as the murmur died down. Everyone was looking at her, waiting to hear what she had to say.

"OK," Sophie said quietly. She paused for a couple of seconds. The classroom was silent. "Let's share and care." She nodded. "How about we do this for Opposite Day? Let's call it a Sharing-Is-Caring Day." Sophie walked to the chalkboard and drew a two-column table:

Sophie	Telescope
Jordan	Game console
Chloe	Makeup kit
Leo	Skateboard
Nancy	Stamp collection
Brian	Karaoke machine
Manu	Walkie-Talkie
Sarah	Camera
Chris	Remote control car
Jamie	Talking robot
Daniel	Airplane model

Sophie continued to list almost everyone in the class, somehow knowing what every one of us could bring.

"Who else?" Sophie turned and asked.

"Oh, David, I almost forgot about your new saxophone." She added him to the list. David, the short, skinny twin who was playing saxophone in the school honor wind ensemble, opened his mouth to say something but didn't. He noticed several looks turning toward him and then closed his mouth slowly.

There was a sense of confusion around the room. Some kids were looking at Nancy, but she just sat in her chair, saying nothing.

"All right, let's vote," Sophie continued. "Who is for bringing our things on Sharing-Is-Caring Day? Please raise your hand."

Sophie raised her hand up high. Two kids in the front immediately raised their hands as well. Everybody was looking around to see what others would do. The fourth, fifth, and sixth hands were raised. Then, slowly, almost everyone did the same.

I looked around—David, Chloe, and Nancy were the only ones with their hands down. And Nancy looked baffled. When more kids started to look around, noticing her hand was still down, she raised her hand as well, and so did Chloe and David.

"Great, now we all know what to bring to Opposite Day so we can share it with everyone else." Sophie walked back to her seat.

The murmur started again. Kids were whispering to one another. Chloe tapped my shoulder and whispered, "Why is she doing this? I don't get it."

"I don't get it either," I replied, turning back to Sophie, who was sitting still in her chair. Right then, our math teacher walked in.

❖ ❖ ❖

And so it was.

When Opposite Day—or, with its new name, Sharing-Is-Caring Day—came about, most of the kids brought their things to the classroom.

Jordan, whose father owned the local supermarket, brought his new gaming console and was terrified when all the boys started fighting over who was going to play it first. Chloe opened her makeup bag and took out brushes, lipsticks, an eyeshadow palette and a little round mirror. A group of girls lined up to have Chloe do their makeup.

Nancy opened her stamp book in the corner of the classroom and made the five kids who were interested in it stand in line before allowing them to touch it. Big Frankie was playing with my skateboard and, for some reason, decided to jump on it with both his feet. As he did, the skateboard slid to the side, and Frankie fell on his hand, hitting the floor hard.

"Are you OK, dude?" I rushed to help him up. Frankie stood, then opened and closed his hand while holding his wrist.

"I'm fine," he said and walked out of the room, his eyebrows pressing down on his eyes. I think he was hurting more than he cared to show.

Sophie set her telescope outside near the basketball court. When I got there to see how things were going, I saw Sophie aiming the telescope at the moon, which was hanging pretty high up in the sky. Jamie and Chris stood next to her. When Sophie finished setting everything up, Jamie rushed to the telescope and looked through its eyepiece.

"Jesus Christ, that's huge," he muttered.

Chris started tapping Jamie on his shoulder. "Come on—let me see!" he yelled.

"Shut up!" Jamie replied. He whipped his hand back while still looking through the telescope, trying to hit Chris who stood right behind him. Chris then pushed Jamie harder. Jamie's face hit the telescope's eyepiece. The telescope tilted from its tripod and started tipping over. I heard Jamie gasp as the telescope began falling toward the ground.

Sophie, who was standing right next to it, immediately jumped to try to stop the fall, reaching for the middle part of the telescope. She managed to get a hold of one of the handles, but it broke off, sending the telescope crashing down to the ground. As it hit the concrete, it made a loud cracking sound.

There was silence all around. Everybody was looking at the telescope as Sophie lifted it from the ground as quickly as she could. She turned it, and we could all see a big crack on the telescope's lens.

Sophie examined the cracked lens quietly and then reached for the bag and slowly wrapped it around the telescope. I was bewildered. Sophie's face was without any expression of anger or sorrow. She just calmly concentrated on the task in front of her.

Jamie pushed Chris with both hands, shouting, "Look what you did!"

Sophie picked up the telescope bag and her sleeping bag and started walking toward the school's front gate.

"Wait!" I called. "Where are you going? We're sleeping in the classroom tonight."

Sophie kept on walking.

I stood there, feeling angry with Jamie and Chris, who started walking back to the school building, yelling at each other. My heart ached as I watched Sophie leave the school grounds carrying the heavy telescope.

I went back to the classroom. It was loud and messy. A group of boys cheered loudly for Jordan, who was playing a karate fighting game on his console. I looked around and saw Chloe sobbing in the corner of the room. Sarah was comforting her while picking up makeup brushes from the floor.

"Hey Chloe, what happened?" I asked and picked up a couple of lipstick tubes that had rolled beneath a chair at the side of the room.

"TM and Brian snatched my bag and started putting on my makeup. They ruined my eyeshadow palette. I spent all my savings on it," Chloe sniffled.

A moment later, I heard Nancy screaming at David for staining her stamp collection with his greasy hands. David looked terrified and embarrassed. He had a slight sweating problem, and nobody would shake his hands because they were always moist.

I felt bad. I thought of Sophie walking home by herself with the broken telescope. I picked up my skateboard and ran out to try to catch up with her. I rode my skateboard as fast as I could until I saw Sophie's figure from afar.

"Soph, wait up!" I yelled.

She turned back to face me, her arms looking like strings hanging down from her shoulders, one holding the telescope bag and the other her sleeping bag.

"Hey, I'm sorry about your telescope," I said as I stopped and got off my skateboard. "Those stupid kids." I shook my head. I didn't know how to comfort her.

We started walking together.

"That's not it," Sophie said in a quiet voice a minute or so later. "It was stupid of me to try to prove a point."

"What do you mean?" I was about to drop my skateboard back to the ground and ride alongside her, but the remark surprised me, so I paused and looked at her.

Sophie didn't answer. I saw a tear coming down from her eye. She stopped walking, laid down her bags, and covered her face with her hands. I could see her face twitching and her chin trembling behind her hands, but she didn't make any sound.

"Hey, I'm sure we can fix the telescope," I said. I put my hand on her shoulder. Sophie sniffled and then took her hands off her face.

"It's not the telescope. It's me. I made it happen, and now I'm paying for it." Sophie wiped her tears away.

"What are you talking about, Sophie? You didn't make anything happen. It was those two idiots fighting over your telescope. Why are you blaming yourself?" I was puzzled.

Sophie picked up her bags and crossed the road toward the shopping center where my mother did her dry cleaning and where there was a small Mexican restaurant I'd never been to before. I followed her, and we sat on one of the benches facing the parking lot.

The afternoon was cloudy and darker than usual. A neon Open sign from the Mexican restaurant painted Sophie's face with a bluish color. She was sitting with her hands on her lap, her fingers intertwined. A car playing loud music drove by with a booming sound that we could hear long after it was out of sight.

It was getting cold, and I felt a heavy, gloomy feeling in my chest.

I looked at Sophie. She was looking down, her eyes darting around as she thought of something.

"Why are you blaming yourself? I don't get it." I moved closer and leaned toward her.

She stood and walked to the end of the pavement, just next to the curb on the side of the road. Sophie squatted next to a small anthill and watched the line of ants going in and out of it.

I walked from the bench and sat down on the curb beside her with the skateboard in my hand. Sophie was quietly observing the ants, her arms hugging her legs.

"Do you think we're like ants, Leo?" Sophie raised her head, still gazing at the ground.

"No, of course not. Why?"

"Because sometimes I feel like I'm expected to act like one." Her face was moving up and down with her chin touching her knees.

"In what way?" I wondered why Sophie would say such a thing.

"At school, we're all learning the same things in the same way. We're expected to share our things with others—just as if we were living in an ant colony, you know?" Her eyes were fixated on the anthill but looking unfocused.

"Maybe we are a little like ants." I shrugged. "And this town is one big colony."

"But we are not!" Sophie stood quickly and threw her hands to her sides. I was startled and looked up, surprised by her reaction.

"We are the exact *opposite* of ants—don't you see?" she exclaimed, pointing at the trail of ants.

"What do you mean by 'the exact opposite'? Why? We live in a society just like they do," I contested, still sitting on the curb and looking up at her.

"Do you know any two people who are exactly the same?" she asked.

I thought for a couple of seconds, looking down at the sidewalk. I tried to think about people who were similar, but I couldn't. It even occurred to me that the identical twins I knew from my father's side of the family just looked alike but were very different from each other.

"No, I don't think so," I replied.

"Now look at those ants...you can't tell one from another." Sophie's hands were both aiming down at the ant trail.

"But what does this have to do with what just happened back at school?" I tried to understand the connection.

"People are not ants—we are free to think for ourselves! We all want different things..." She paused and sat down next to me. Sophie thought for a long minute before she started talking again.

"Look, when I suggested that all of us in class bring our most valuable things to school, I thought that they would be smart enough to disagree and reject the idea. Remember what happened when I asked everyone to vote?"

"Yes, a couple of kids raised their hands and...then...I guess everyone followed," I recalled.

"Right. It was peer pressure. People were afraid to look selfish and raised their hands even though they didn't want to."

I was listening carefully to what Sophie was saying, trying to understand where she was going with this.

"And when they all raised their hands, instead of explaining why it was all wrong, I decided to just...let it happen." Sophie turned to me with her piercing look again.

"Let *what* happen?" I was still not quite following her.

"What happens when you force people to share because someone said it is the right thing to do—a disaster. Chris and Jamie don't care about telescopes, so they were not as careful as I would be—and this is the result." Sophie pointed back at the telescope bag.

Then she leaned toward me and started talking as if disclosing a secret. "Why is sharing always the right thing to do? What if I don't want to share? Is it bad because I am supposed to care about other people more than I care about myself? Why should I? It doesn't make any sense."

"But then everyone would be selfish and mean," I argued.

Sophie leaned back and spoke a little louder. "No, they wouldn't. Well first, let's be clear what 'selfish' means. Being selfish means to care for *yourself*. I think that it would be great if everybody did what's genuinely best for *themselves*. Not by mindlessly hurting other people—that is the *opposite* of being selfish. Being selfish and being mean to people is not the same thing. In most cases they are opposites. You should do things that are good *for you*, including sharing stuff with other people, but only because *you* care about them or because it is somehow helping *you*."

The wind suddenly blew harder, and when I looked up to the cloudy sky, I knew it wouldn't be long before it started raining. I turned to look back at Sophie and saw she was still looking down, shaking her head slightly.

"Hmm..." I scratched the back of my head. "So you're saying that making everyone bring their things to school was wrong?"

"Yes, that's what I'm saying. When people choose to share or exchange stuff, then both sides usually win. Like how we got paid, and our customers got a clean yard. Or like the kid that bought your comic book. It's a winwin—both sides get something. But when you're expected to share and give, not by choice, but by pressure or force, then it is either a win-lose or even a lose-lose." Sophie looked at me.

I looked back at her, trying to digest everything she was saying. It wasn't easy, and I felt a bit confused. She was right about the fact that most of what happened earlier looked like a win-lose or a lose-lose.

"So what did you gain when you decided to share your telescope with me the other day?" I was not clear why Sophie claimed that every time someone shared something they were supposed to get something in return.

"I got to spend time with you. To see you enjoy it. Together with me." Sophie smiled. "You're great—you know that?" Sophie's smile got even bigger, the corners of her mouth curling upward.

"Me?" I was not seeing what was so great about me at that particular moment.

"Yes, you're listening to me blabbering about my thoughts, and...you listen. You care." Sophie brushed her hand against my shoulder and turned back toward the bench behind us. She picked up her bags and tilted her head toward the other side of the road. "I'm going to go back home."

"Wait, let me get this straight—you knew that this evening would end up a disaster?" I asked as I got up and stood in front of her.

"In a way." She nodded.

"You are strange, Sophie." I shook my head.

"I think I agree with you." Sophie smiled and started crossing the street. I followed her, and we headed back to our neighborhood.

"Let me carry the telescope...and I am doing it for *me*." I smirked.

"Oh, now you're talking." She smiled back and handed me her bag.

I noticed Sophie's smile had suddenly disappeared.

"What's wrong?" I asked.

"I think I made a mistake. I can't draw that kind of attention..." She paused.

"Because of the immigration issue?" I asked.

Sophie nodded. We got close to her house, and she reached for the telescope bag I was carrying.

"I'll see you tomorrow." Sophie flung the telescope bag over her shoulder, opened the front gate, and entered her house.

Standing on the other side of her gate, I felt again what I'd felt the first time I met Sophie: I was curious about that girl.

I thought of walking back home but then realized I had left my sleeping bag at school and that my parents were not expecting me to come home that night. I decided to go back and sleep at school with my classmates.

When I got there, I saw Frankie and some other boys shouting on one side of the classroom, and the girls huddled together in one of the corners, giggling. Mr. Sumner and another teacher came around to check that we were getting ready to go to sleep.

I quickly learned that the mouthpiece of David's saxophone had broken as well and that Chloe had gone home with her mother with her broken makeup kit. Before Chloe left, she screamed at Nancy that this whole "sharing" idea was awful and that it was all her fault. Other kids joined the argument, and Nancy got deeply hurt—so much so that, later, her mother came to pick her up as well. Several other parents who came to visit and heard what had happened got pretty upset.

When most of the kids had fallen asleep in their sleeping bags, it got quieter, and I could hear the rain outside. I started thinking about Sophie and what she had said earlier.

I wonder what the world would look like if being selfish was considered a good thing was my last thought before I fell asleep.

CHAPTER 11

GRAVITY AND PULL

The next morning, Mr. Sumner woke us up. We stood in a line to wash our faces and brush our teeth in the restrooms. Then we had breakfast that several parent volunteers had made for us in the cafeteria. The students who hadn't slept in class came in later that morning, and the social studies class that followed was boring as usual.

"Look at this." Sophie showed me a crumpled piece of paper as we left the classroom for recess. I opened the note, which said, "I know exactly what you did yesterday. You'll get what you deserve!" The handwriting was tidy and round, and I immediately recognized it.

"Nancy," I said.

"Yes," Sophie replied with half a smile.

As we passed the front office on our way out of the building, Ms. White came walking out, just as she had the last time Sophie had been summoned to the social committee.

"Sophia Anwar?" she asked as she got closer to us.

Sophie and I turned to face Ms. White. She was waiting for Sophie to respond, but Sophie just looked back at her. After a quick second of silence, Ms. White looked edgy again, precisely as she had the last time.

"Oh, uh…Sophie, Principal Palmer needs you to see him after school." She rubbed her hands together.

"What about?" Sophie replied in a tone that seemed to make Ms. White even more uncomfortable.

"I…I don't really know, dear. Please just come over to the office after your last period with Mr. Sumner, OK?" Ms. White said, and she turned back to the front office.

"I wonder if this is about last night," I said, as we walked through the main entrance and out of the building. Sophie nodded and pointed to an open bench.

❖   ❖   ❖

Mr. Sumner's class that day was fascinating. We learned about gravity and how objects attract one another. Mr. Sumner had brought a large, elastic piece of fabric and had us all stand and hold it, so it was stretched and tight. Then he took out a ball and rolled it onto the surface. Everybody giggled as the ball circled from one side to the other. The ball finally rested in the middle of the fabric.

"Space is like this fabric," Mr. Sumner said as he walked around us, his hands behind his back. "It is elastic, and it bends around objects with mass. Imagine that this ball is the sun. You can see how the space around it is curved. Now, look what happens to a planet, like Earth, if it gets closer to the warped space around the sun." He then rolled a marble around the edge of the tight fabric. The marble rolled and started circling the bigger ball in tightening circles.

"This is why Earth and the other planets orbit the sun. Who can tell me where the moon would fit in this model?"

Daniel shouted the answer. "It would be an even smaller marble circling the big marble." He got a little too excited, and his voice cracked. Everyone laughed.

"We have a young Einstein here." Mr. Sumner smiled, patting Daniel on his back.

Right then, Mr. Palmer opened the classroom door. He looked at all of us standing in the middle of the class and then scanned the desks and chairs pushed to the edges of the room.

"What's all this?" Mr. Palmer seemed irritated to see the messy classroom.

"We're experimenting," Mr. Sumner replied quickly, smiling.

"This is not a lab, Mr. Sumner. Can I have a word with you outside, please?" Mr. Palmer closed the door, and I could see his angry face through the door's narrow window.

Mr. Sumner went out of the classroom. Big Frankie, Jamie, and Chris ran to the door to try to hear what was going on in the hall. I joined them. We were all cramped against the door, squatting beneath the door's narrow window.

We could hear Mr. Palmer talk, but it was hard to understand what he was saying. And then, unexpectedly, we heard Mr. Sumner talking back loudly to Mr. Palmer. I'd never heard Mr. Sumner get angry, but he was definitely irritated.

"Are you kidding me? They love this. I'm not teaching by reading from a book! You're asking me to make science boring, just like all other classes!"

We heard steps coming our way, and immediately all of us who were eavesdropping rushed back to the middle of the classroom.

Mr. Sumner opened the door and stood there, looking at all of us with a severe look.

"All right, kids," he finally said after a long moment. "Put everything back in place, and then you're dismissed for the day."

I looked back at Sophie. She looked disappointed.

After we finished organizing the desks and chairs back in their rows, I walked to the back of the classroom.

"They have to be crazy if they think that he is doing something wrong." Sophie shook her head as she put a book back in her plastic bag.

"Well, you have to admit he is a little different in the way he teaches," I said.

"Yes, he is different for sure."

"So are you going to Mr. Palmer's office? He doesn't seem to be in a good mood today." I grinned.

"I guess I have to. I bet this time they're going to nail me for Opposite Day," she answered calmly. I thought I was probably more worried about that meeting than she was.

When we got to the front office, Ms. White was on the phone. As we stood there waiting, I noticed that Mr. Palmer's office door was open. I moved to my left and saw Mrs. Sanders standing inside, talking to Mr. Palmer.

She was dressed up in a blue suit with her blond hair combed neatly as if every strand of hair knew its place.

Ms. White finished the phone call and turned to Sophie.

"You can sit here, dear. Mr. Palmer will see you in the boardroom in a minute."

Sophie sat down on the wooden bench attached to the wall just in front of Ms. White's desk. I stood next to her.

"Aren't you going to eavesdrop again?" Sophie whispered, looking up at me.

"You bet I am," I replied, and I walked out of the office.

As I found my place below the boardroom's window, I heard Mrs. Sanders's deep, cigarette-heavy voice: "How are you, Sophie?"

"I'm fine," I heard Sophie answer in a monotone voice.

I heard chairs moving, and then Mr. Palmer started talking. "Ms. Anwar, we want to talk to you about two different things. First," he said in a relaxed and joyful tone that surprised me, "we have the results of the standardized tests everyone took last month. Your score was quite remarkable."

Mr. Palmer paused.

"OK," Sophie replied flatly.

"Don't you want to know how you scored?" Ingrid Sanders interjected.

"I don't know. Is it important?" Sophie asked unenthusiastically.

"It is very important for you and our school." Mr. Palmer sounded pleased. "You scored the highest in the entire state, Sophie. You should be proud of yourself. I guess you're paying attention in class—that is super."

There was no reply.

"We might ask you to take a couple of pictures for the school once we get the formal results," Mr. Palmer added, and it sounded like he waited for a response that didn't come.

"OK, we have one more issue to talk about. Would you mind telling us about what exactly happened yesterday at Opposite Day? We heard different stories about it." Mr. Palmer's voice sounded more formal and dry.

Sophie responded rather quickly. "Well, last week, after some kids in class thought that I should share my telescope with everyone—just because I have one—I suggested that if we're expected to share our valuable things, we might as well share them all as part of Opposite Day."

"That's an interesting idea," I heard Ingrid Sanders comment. It sounded like she was smiling or pleased with what Sophie had just said.

"So you suggested that everyone bring something valuable and share it with others?" Mr. Palmer asked.

"I did," Sophie replied.

"Why did you do that?" Mrs. Sanders asked curiously.

Several seconds of silence went by, and I was tempted to peek and see what was going on but didn't want to risk getting caught. Then finally, Sophie started talking again. "I did it to make a point."

"Make a point? What point?" Mr. Palmer sounded surprised.

"That it is wrong to demand that people share their things because other people need or want them. I—"

"Wait a minute," Ingrid Sanders interrupted. "I want to make sure I understand. You did it because you think that it is *wrong* for people to share what they have with other people?"

There was a short pause again. *Please don't go there, Soph*, I thought, right when I heard Sophie doing the exact opposite thing.

"Well, it depends," she said. "I think it is fine if people want to share something they have with people they care about, but I think it is wrong to *force* them to do it when it is not in their best interest."

Suddenly I heard laughter. Ingrid Sanders started laughing, and a quick second later, Mr. Palmer joined with a weird-sounding chuckle.

"You're quite naive, little girl. It doesn't work like that in the real world," Ingrid Sanders said in a condescending voice.

"So you admit you had an active part in causing all the commotion we had yesterday at Opposite Day? Some kids and parents got pretty upset last night," Mr. Palmer asked in a severe tone.

"Yes." Sophie didn't hesitate with her reply.

"I want you to think long and hard about it and make sure you learn from this experience." Mr. Palmer sounded formal, as if he was reading from a script.

"I already did," Sophie replied.

"Good, so consider this as a warning. You're dismissed, Ms. Anwar, and I hope you don't get involved in other incidents like this one in the future," Mr. Palmer said.

I heard a chair being pulled back, and a couple of seconds later, the door opened and closed. I thought about crawling away from there and running to meet Sophie around the building, but then I heard Ingrid Sanders talking again.

"Smart girl. I heard she built a website for the school all by herself." Ingrid sounded impressed.

"Indeed, and it is pretty good. Sumner showed it to me. The thing is that there is no way that the school board would approve for us to use it. In the last meeting, they said that there is a plan to have a standard website template for all the city schools. But if you ask me, it'll take them years to make it happen," Mr. Palmer complained.

"Yes, I know what you mean, Robert. Regardless, that girl continues to surprise me."

"Well—" Mr. Palmer tried to respond, but he didn't get a chance.

Mrs. Sanders continued, "Now call Sumner in—we have to stop this guy from making all the other teachers look bad."

I heard chairs moving and the door opening again. I wanted to catch up with Sophie, but I was too curious to know what was going on with Mr. Sumner. I looked around to make sure no one was watching me sitting just below the window's frame.

"Mr. Sumner," Mr. Palmer started, "this is the third time we are meeting on this matter. Your methods of teaching continue to be out of compliance with the school's and the county's guidelines. We hear constant complaints, and we must put an end to this." Mr. Palmer sounded stern.

"Give me a name of *one* student who complained about my lessons." Mr. Sumner sounded irritated.

There was a short pause, and suddenly I heard leaves rustling in the bushes next to me. I was about to jump and run, thinking someone had caught me, but soon enough Sophie's face appeared behind the bush.

"Shh..." I put my finger to my lips and signaled her to keep low with my other hand. As Sophie settled down next to me, we heard Mr. Sumner talking again.

"I bet you can't name one. All those so-called complaints are coming from other teachers who won't make an effort to make their lessons engaging and interesting. Am I right?"

"You are out of line, Mr. Sumner," Mrs. Sanders said. "The fact is that you are not following the public-school board guidelines and curriculum, and that cannot be tolerated. You can't just teach how and what you like. That's not how our system works."

"And who made those guidelines? Who are they good for?" I was surprised with how Mr. Sumner answered Mrs. Sanders. "Look, I love what I do. I love seeing the kids enjoy my lessons, my stories, and the games we play. They remember every little detail about the subjects because I make it contextual and fun. But your system and your guidelines, made by bureaucrats sitting in government offices, are not about the students. They are about protecting the system itself!" Mr. Sumner's voice broke.

"That's absurd! What would happen if all our teachers decided for themselves what and how to teach? We would have chaos!" Mr. Palmer responded.

"We would have innovation and progress," Mr. Sumner replied rather quietly.

There was another short pause. Sophie and I looked at each other. Sophie's eyebrows were raised, creating wrinkles in her forehead. I couldn't tell if she was surprised, confused, or angry.

"This place is obviously not for you, Mr. Sumner," Mrs. Sanders said calmly.

"You're right. It's not. You'll have my resignation letter as soon as I finish the current unit," Mr. Sumner replied, and the sound of a chair pushed back told us he was leaving the room.

Sophie immediately crawled to the side of the window toward the bushes, and I followed her.

FREE MONEY

The next Thursday was a teacher's workday, which meant no school. Sophie and I decided to meet next to our tree at noon. Sophie was leaning on the tree when I got there. She was looking at her hands. It looked like she had blisters on both of them.

"Is that from your cleaning work?" I asked.

"Yes, they have this wooden mop that's killing me." She raised her head and looked at me.

"I don't even know how often you work there. You're all hush-hush about it," I said.

"Well, I guess I can tell you, but please don't tell anyone, and don't come visit me there. It would be too risky."

"Of course," I nodded.

"I work in the Mediterranean restaurant in the Cummins strip mall near the ice cream place. I work most afternoons and evenings now." Sophie was back to scratching a blister on the palm of her hand.

"Is the new work paying as well as you thought it would?" I asked.

"It is. The owner paid me a bonus because he said I work fast. I saved a thousand dollars and gave it to the lawyer already. So he's got four thousand out of the five he needs for the immigration status process. Getting closer..." Sophie raised her head again and pushed herself up from leaning on the tree.

I could see Sophie was hopeful, and it made me happy.

"Hey," she said, getting a little closer to me. "Do you want to come over to my house for lunch? My mother is feeling better, and she made something special."

"Really?" I was surprised. During all the months since I'd met her, in the dozens of times we'd talked in front of her house, Sophie had never invited me in.

"Yes, my mother made delicious meat dumplings that you have to try. Let's go." Sophie extended her hand toward mine. I put my hand in hers, and we walked to her house.

Sophie opened the door, and we went in. The house was smaller than it looked from the outside, and the ceiling was noticeably low. As we walked in, I could see the living room that had an old sofa and a coffee table with several folded shirts on it. There was no TV, and I saw no pictures on the walls. It looked kind of empty. There was one small table at the corner of the living room with what looked like a sewing machine.

To the left of the front door was a kitchen with brown wooden cabinets and a white refrigerator much smaller than the usual size. The kitchen looked old but was clean and tidy. One of the cabinet doors was missing, and I noticed the cabinet was empty.

There were two pots on the stove, and the aroma that came from the kitchen smelled like peppers. It was spicy and fresh.

Sophie's mother came out of the short hall, which appeared to lead to two bedrooms. I noticed she wasn't wearing a gown; instead, she had on a simple shirt and a pair of beige pants. She looked better in this standard outfit. Her face was whiter than I remembered, and her eyes were big and green. She was a beautiful woman—even more so from up close.

She smiled at me, bowed her head slightly, and went straight to the kitchen. Sophie went toward her room, and I followed her.

As I walked down the short hall behind Sophie, we passed her mother's bedroom. I saw a single bed and a small dresser topped with many little bottles that looked like medicines. On the other side of the bed was a big tank with a plastic tube coming out of it that said "oxygen."

Then we went into Sophie's room. It was a small room with a big, brown wardrobe that took up most of the room's space. There was no bed, just a mattress on the floor that was pushed into the corner of the room. Sophie didn't have a desk either, only a chair with a pair of shoes beneath it.

A pile of books was stacked next to the head of the mattress with the top one open. Most of the books had little pieces of paper sticking out of them. There was a small lamp on the floor, and its cord ran all the way to an outlet on the other side of the room.

"Welcome to my little part of the world." Sophie smiled, opening her hands in a welcoming gesture. We stood in the middle of the room, which felt both empty and cozy at the same time.

"I love this room—it is quiet and has a lot of light coming from this window." She pointed at the window above the mattress.

We sat down on the mattress, which had a neatly folded blanket on it.

"What is this language?" I pointed at the book on the top of the pile.

Sophie picked the book up and showed it to me. "It's Arabic. It's one of the few books my grandfather put in my suitcase before we left. He told me to read them when I'm older, but I couldn't wait." Sophie's voice trembled a little.

"What is it about?" I inquired.

"A hero. Someone who knows what he wants out of life and does everything he can to make it happen with no compromises. A little like your Orthea." Sophie leaned toward me and nudged my shoulder with hers.

"Hey, what do you think about Mr. Sumner?" I asked, as we hadn't gotten to talk about it after what we overheard in the committee.

Sophie didn't say anything. It seemed as though she had something to say but chose not to. We heard Sophie's mother call Sophie's name and then say something in Arabic from the kitchen.

Sophie closed the book, laid it on top of the pile, and said, "Come—it's time to eat."

Sophie's mother was sitting on a chair in the living room, and a plate of dumplings and rice in red sauce was on the little coffee table. Next to it was a plastic water bottle with plastic cups.

The meat dumplings were like nothing I'd ever tasted before. They were made of something that looked like grits, but their texture was different. Inside there was a mix of minced onions and ground meat that tasted so good that I took another one without even asking. Sophie showed me how to mix the rice with the red sauce, which made the dish even more delicious.

"This is so good." I pointed at the dumplings after noticing that both Sophie and her mother were watching me, smiling.

"It's called kibbeh." Sophie giggled.

Suddenly, there was a knock on the door. Sophie's mother glanced at Sophie with a concerned look.

"It's OK, Mama." Sophie touched her mother's knee and went to open the door.

"Mrs. Sanders?" Sophie said, looking at the open door. "What are you doing here?"

I couldn't hear the answer, but Sophie stepped back, and Ingrid Sanders walked in. Sophie's mother stood, and so did I.

Ingrid Sanders was scanning the house as she walked in, and then her eyes landed on Sophie's mother and me. Her sharp-looking blue suit, her high-heeled shoes, and the low ceiling made her look even taller than usual. She was holding a little white purse that had a handle made of pearls.

"Oh, it's so very nice to meet you." Ingrid Sanders walked straight to Sophie's mother with her hand extended for a handshake. Sophie's mother hesitated but then reached to shake Ingrid's hand.

"And you—good to see you too, Leo." Ingrid patted my head in a way that made me feel like a little boy.

"Sorry I came without prior notice, Mrs. Anwar," Ingrid continued. She sat down on the sofa next to where I was standing.

"She can't understand what you're saying. She doesn't speak English," Sophie said as she closed the door. Sophie's mother sat down back in her chair, looking a little anxious and confused. Sophie walked back and stood in front of the sofa, next to her mother. One of her hands rested on her mother's shoulder, and her eyes were focused on Ingrid, looking very alert.

The whole situation felt awkward, and I didn't know what to do. I stood to the side of the sofa, next to Ingrid, and swallowed the last bite of the kibbeh I had in my mouth.

"So you may be wondering why I am here," Ingrid said with a broad smile, clasping her hands together and looking straight at Mrs. Anwar.

Sophie translated what Ingrid was saying to her mother, whispering in her ear. It took too long for the short sentence that Ingrid had just said, so I assumed Sophie was also explaining to her mother what was going on. After Sophie finished, she looked back at Ingrid.

"I'm here to tell you that I've done a little bit of research, and as I understand, your mother is not working, and your father is not living with you. Is that correct?" Ingrid was still looking around the house as she spoke, as if gathering more information.

Sophie became uneasy when Ingrid uttered those words. Her eyebrows scrunched together, making her look like she was frowning, almost annoyed. I was concerned that Ingrid had found out about their immigration issue.

"That's correct," Sophie replied.

Ingrid nodded and looked like she was expecting more details from Sophie, but Sophie just kept looking straight at Ingrid without blinking.

There was a long pause, and I felt the tension building in the room. Sophie was looking at Ingrid. Sophie's mother had a worried look on her face, and her eyes darted between Sophie and Ingrid. Ingrid, on the other hand, looked calm and had a smug smile on her face as if she knew something we didn't.

After a long, awkward pause, Ingrid lowered her purse to the floor and whispered, pointing at Sophie's mother, "And I also know about your condition, Mrs. Anwar, but I wanted you to know that you are in good hands."

Sophie leaned forward. "How do you know about my mother's condition?" Sophie asked in a suspicious tone.

"That's not the point. The point is that I'm here to help you both. Do you know what welfare and entitlement programs are?" Ingrid was still smiling.

"Yes," Sophie answered. "It is tax money the government gives to poor people."

"That's a wrong way to think about it. It is help for people in need," Ingrid corrected Sophie. "And I know a thing or two about those programs. I managed those on our city council."

Ingrid turned to Mrs. Anwar. "You could get some food stamps, help with your rent, and even some allowance for your expenses."

I listened carefully to what Ingrid was saying and started to think Sophie *could* use some help taking care of her mother while she saved for the lawyer's fee.

Sophie translated to her mother. Mrs. Anwar turned to look at Sophie while Sophie looked back at Ingrid. A wrinkle in Sophie's forehead hinted that she was concerned or worried...or maybe just trying to figure out what was going on.

After a long moment, Sophie wrapped her hand around her mother's shoulder and said, "We don't need food stamps or any kind of handouts, Mrs. Sanders. We're doing fine."

Ingrid tilted her head sideways in surprise.

What are you thinking? a voice in my head shouted at Sophie.

"It's not a handout, dear; it is just a little help. And besides..." Ingrid looked around the living room. "I'd say you *do* need some help."

Mrs. Anwar raised her hand to touch Sophie's sleeve. She wanted Sophie to translate what was going on, but Sophie continued. "We have what we need, Mrs. Sanders," Sophie said in a formal tone.

Ingrid Sanders's face softened, and she leaned forward. "Sophie, I know you're a proud girl, and I admire that about you, but I just want to help you and make sure you get what you deserve. We care for one another around here, you know?"

I was looking at Sophie. I was thinking how much she needed the money. I knew Sophie sometimes struggled to make enough to buy basic groceries.

"I prefer to work and make my own money," Sophie replied.

I could see Ingrid was surprised yet again by that response. She sat tall in her chair and looked straight at Sophie with a piercing look. "Thirteen-year-old girls should not be working. Especially someone as smart as you." Ingrid paused, turned to Sophie's mother, and continued, "Look, I know this is tough for you both, and I hope you know I'm here to help. So just think about it, OK?"

Sophie didn't reply. Sophie and Ingrid were looking straight at each other now.

"Wait," Ingrid said suddenly, raising her index finger in the air as if she'd just thought of something. "So you just said you want to work, right?"

Sophie still didn't say anything. I didn't think Ingrid knew Sophie was already working.

"Perhaps we can do something a little different," Ingrid said with a sly look on her face. "I heard you've built a pretty good website for the school. How about you build a website for my election campaign? I will pay you, of course."

Sophie thought for a second. She looked down at her mother and then glanced at me before looking back at Ingrid. "Alright, I can do that." Sophie nodded, her face still sealed, not showing any emotion.

"Great," Ingrid said. She stood, lifting her purse from its pearl-braided handle and straightening her suit's jacket. "Would you mind coming over to our house tomorrow afternoon?" Ingrid smiled as she turned toward the door. Mrs. Anwar stood up as well, but Ingrid didn't look at her. She focused on Sophie, who moved toward the door as well.

"I'm busy tomorrow, but I can come over Saturday afternoon, if that's OK." Sophie looked up at Ingrid as she passed her on her way to the entrance.

"That'll be fine. See you Saturday afternoon at four? I'm sure you know where I live. Everyone does." Ingrid chuckled and turned to face the door Sophie had opened.

"See you soon." Ingrid waved and walked out toward her car, which was parked outside the gate. Sophie, her mother, and I were all standing by the door, watching Ingrid Sanders get into her car and drive away.

We went back inside and sat in our chairs in the living room. Mrs. Anwar, whom I hadn't heard speaking much until that point, started asking Sophie question after question in Arabic. Sophie seemed to get annoyed but answered in what sounded like a polite, quiet tone.

Mrs. Anwar continued and was now talking to Sophie in a louder voice, pointing her finger at her.

As Mrs. Anwar was talking, now almost yelling, I noticed Sophie was getting upset, her jaw tensing up and her eyebrows knotting, creating a little furrow between them.

I was sure she was about to respond, but instead, she stood up, grabbed me by the hand, and muttered in an angry voice, "It's always about the money, isn't it? Let's get out of here."

She pulled me toward the door as I looked disappointedly at the half-full plate of kibbeh I would never get to finish. Sophie slammed the door behind us while Mrs. Anwar was still shouting in Arabic.

We went straight to the oak tree.

Sophie sat down with her back against the trunk and her eyes looking far into the horizon. I sat down next to her. I picked up a dry, narrow branch and started chipping its bark off.

"That was weird." I reclined back to my elbows and extended my legs forward on the patch of grass.

"I don't think it was weird at all." Sophie's eyes were still looking far, thinking.

"You know I don't like Ingrid Sanders, but why won't you let her help you? Sounds like she wants to give you some free money, so why not take it? She is a powerful figure around here, you know?"

Sophie turned her head and looked at me. "Do you think she wants to help me? Do you think there is such a thing as 'free money' from someone like Ingrid Sanders? And did you ask yourself what would be the price I pay for that so-called 'free money'?" Sophie stood quickly.

I stood as well and dropped the little branch I was holding.

"I need some time to myself. I'll see you tomorrow, Leo," Sophie said. She walked away toward the park.

"Why are you so stubborn?" I yelled at her as she was walking away. Sophie didn't turn and just lowered her head, increasing her pace.

CHAPTER 13

THE WHITE HOUSE

I t was Saturday morning. I was lying in my bed, enjoying the warmth of the sun on my back—I always kept a narrow crack in my window curtains to allow a ray of sunlight to wake me up gently.

I thought about Sophie. *Why isn't she willing to bend her beliefs a little and take the money Ingrid Sanders mentioned? What harm could it do? Is Sophie being reasonable about this whole thing?*

I got dressed and went down to grab some cereal for breakfast. My father was reading his newspaper at the breakfast table.

"Where's Mom?" I asked, stuffing my mouth with cornflakes.

"She's out helping with the Sanders campaign." He exhaled, shook his head, and turned another page of his newspaper.

I finished my cereal and put the bowl in the sink. "See you later, Dad," I said on my way to the front door.

"Don't break anything," I heard him say just as the door closed behind me.

I knocked on Sophie's front door and took a step back. Sophie opened it.

"Hey, you. Are you OK?" I asked, putting my hands in my pockets.

"Yes, I'm fine. I was just about to leave for work. Then I have to go to Ingrid's house. I got the address. Looks like quite a walk."

"I haven't been there, but I know where it is. It's over on the west side, where the big ranches are. Are you nervous?" I looked at Sophie's face, knowing the idea of working for Mrs. Sanders could be difficult for her.

"I'm not. I'm planning to build her a website and get paid for it. It's business—that's all. See you when I'm back?" Sophie asked, and I nodded.

"Six thirty by the tree?"

"I'll be there," I said, and turned to walk away. I stepped down from Sophie's porch and started walking toward the park. I turned around and saw Sophie still standing on her porch, her arms crossed, watching me as I walked.

"What?" I cried back at her.

Her little smile broadened across her face.

"Nothing," Sophie yelled back.

At six thirty we met by the oak tree.

"So? How did it go?" I inquired.

"Ingrid wants me to build a website for her campaign and her foundation. It's called The Good Shepherd."

"Really? That's cool. I know The Good Shepherd. My mother volunteers there from time to time."

The Good Shepherd was a very well-known organization. Our congregation often handed flyers for its fund-raising events around in church, and we even got a monthly newsletter in the mail.

Sophie still seemed to be bothered by something. She wasn't smiling and showed no excitement. She was leaning on the tree trunk looking preoccupied with a thought.

"What's wrong?" I asked, getting a little closer to her.

"I need that money," Sophie said quietly and crossed her arms over her chest.

"Go on—spit it out," I said, knowing Sophie would not be concerned without a good reason.

Sophie looked down, moving the tip of her shoe back and forth, making a little arc in the dirt below her. "The lawyer said that if I don't come up with the money and start the immigration status change process, we could get deported at any moment. It will only take for someone to report us, and..." Sophie paused again.

"Go on," I urged her.

"I'm still a thousand dollars short. I asked Ingrid for five hundred for the website, and she agreed. With that money and a little bit more from what I can save in the next several weeks, I should be able to make it...and if we start the immigration process, we should be safe."

"That's great, Soph!" I felt relieved and didn't understand why Sophie didn't seem to be more optimistic, now that she had a path to pay for the lawyer.

"Probably, but it will take about six weeks to save the rest. I hope that's enough time."

The following week, Sophie concentrated on building the website for Ingrid Sanders. She was reading computer books during classes and drawing all sorts of designs in her notebook. Every free moment she had off from work she spent in front of the library computer.

In about a week and a half, Sophie finished her work. She came into class holding two books and touched my shoulder as she passed by my desk. I looked up and saw her grinning.

"What?" I looked back at her as she continued to walk toward the back of the classroom.

"I finished the website. It's published." Sophie looked back at me, pleased.

I wanted to say something, but then I heard the class door closing. Mr. Sumner came in. He wasn't smiling as he usually did. Instead, he looked troubled.

I sat up straight in my chair and turned quickly to look at Sophie. Her face suddenly became bitter, her eyebrows, eyelids, and the edges of her mouth dropping. She knew, as I did, what was about to happen.

"Kids," Mr. Sumner said. He clasped his hands together in front of his face and closed his eyes as if getting ready for a prayer. "I have some not-so-good news to share with you." He bowed his head and opened his eyes. "I will not be teaching you anymore."

"What? Why?" Several kids gasped, and there was a loud murmur around the room.

"The school management and I cannot agree on some things, and so...I will have to leave. I will miss you all...you are amazing kids, and I enjoyed teaching you very much. So stay curious, and I hope some of you will, one day, become scientists...great scientists." Mr. Sumner picked up his note-book from the desk and turned to walk out. His face did not show any tension or anger— he just looked sad. Purely sad.

"No, this is not fair." Chloe stood up next to me as Mr. Sumner got ready to open the door.

He slowly turned back toward the class. "Not everything in life is fair, and we all need to learn how to deal with it." I noticed a silent, single tear rolling down Mr. Sumner's cheek. "Take care, kids," he said quietly, and left the classroom.

After school, I walked with Sophie to the library.

We walked without talking for most of the way there. As we were climbing up the hill, Sophie turned to me and said, "It is interesting what Mr. Sumner said before he left class today."

"Which part?"

"The part about learning how to deal with things that happen to you, even if they are unfair."

"Yeah." I nodded. "He didn't deserve this."

"I think he is right," Sophie continued. "There is a lot to learn about how to deal with tough things."

I was not sure I understood what she meant. We entered the library, and Sophie walked toward the corner of the room where the computers were. She sat down and pulled out a chair for me as well.

"I need to go to Ingrid's house tomorrow and show her the website. It is published and ready to go. Will you come with me?" Sophie asked in a gentle voice.

"Are we riding the bike or walking there?"

"Let's walk." Sophie smiled and turned to face the computer.

Sophie showed me the website she'd built. I didn't know much about websites, but it was clear, elegant, and well structured. I left the library soon after, and Sophie stayed to "fix a couple of things."

❖ ❖ ❖

We met near the oak tree the next afternoon. I pulled out the morning newspaper that I tucked beneath my armpit, and I handed it to Sophie.

"Did you see that? You're famous now." I pointed to the main page, which had Sophie's picture together with Mr. Palmer and Mrs. Sanders.

"What?" Sophie was surprised and grabbed the newspaper out of my hands. She examined the picture carefully. "They took this picture just a couple of days ago at school. They never mentioned they were going to put it in the paper! I thought it was for Mr. Palmer's office or something. So stupid of me!" Sophie's arms dropped, the paper in her hand making a rustling sound. She threw her head back and closed her eyes in frustration. She handed me back the paper.

"Sanders is taking our education to the next level," the headline said. The article mentioned that a thirteen-year-old girl had scored the highest score ever recorded in the state's standardized test. It didn't mention Sophie's name.

"You can rub this in Nancy's face," I joked.

"This is not funny, Leo," Sophie said. "I can't be exposed like this—it's dangerous." She shook her head, took a deep breath, and closed her eyes again. When she opened them, she suddenly looked calmer and more relaxed. "I can't let this get in my way now. I have to get the money from Ingrid. Shall we go?"

We walked for almost an hour. The road to the Sanders family's house was winding through open fields and fenced ranches that stretched for miles. In one of the farms we passed, we saw a herd of horses galloping through the grassy meadow, so we took a little break and climbed onto the bottom rail of the white fence to watch them.

As we passed the big church, we got to a road that was shaded with two rows of big trees, making it look like a big tunnel of leaves. At the end of that path was a tall black gate leading to a gray gravel driveway.

Sophie pressed the intercom button on a white panel that hung on the wall to the right of the gate. The gate opened, making a humming sound, and we followed the driveway, which had a row of green cypress trees on each side of it. The road bent to the left, and slowly a large white house revealed itself behind the trees.

"Wow," I said. "I didn't realize Nancy was already living in the White House."

Sophie laughed.

As we got closer to the house, a rather large woman with a white apron was waiting for us at the front door. She showed us in, and we walked through the entrance hall, which had a high ceiling and a massive crystal chandelier hanging from a thick gold chain.

The woman led us to a sitting area near Ingrid Sanders's home office. Two big, old chairs with detailed wooden carvings sat on a red carpet, making the room look like it was part of a royal palace. Their fabric seemed so soft and silky that I had to brush my hand on one of them as we passed by. The woman asked us to sit on a couple of chairs that stood against the wall on the side of the room and wait for Mrs. Sanders.

There were several paintings on the walls, including an enormous one right in front of us. Its vast white canvas had splashes of color on it, and I tried to figure out what they meant. I looked at Sophie and saw that she was looking at the same painting.

"This drives me crazy," I said.

"Why?" She smiled.

"This is not art. Whoever painted it is a..." I was looking for a word.

"Is a what?" Sophie seemed curious.

"A fraud," I finally said, nodding. I was pleased to find the right word to express what I meant.

"A fraud? Why?" Sophie asked, still looking at the big painting.

"Because it makes you think it is a piece of art, but it isn't. It pretends to mean something, and it doesn't." I raised my hands in the air and then dropped them, making a patting sound on my thighs.

"Hmm...that's an interesting thought." Sophie turned her head toward me slowly.

"For me, art needs to express something that people can connect to, and it needs to mean something. Something that you want to express as an artist." I thought of how inspiring David Brankow's drawings were to me.

Sophie smiled a big smile and turned in her chair to face me. "My grandfather was an art collector, and his house was filled with paintings and sculptures. Mainly sculptures." Sophie's eyes gazed unfocused above my head. I could see she was envisioning her grandfather's house.

"What kind of sculptures?" I asked.

"Of people. They looked like Greek gods and were mostly...naked." She giggled, and her eyes snapped back to reality as they landed on me. "One of them was carrying the globe on his shoulders, and it made me feel like anything was possible. Like a single man has the power to change the world."

Right then, the double doors of Ingrid's office opened, and Ingrid came out. Behind her, I saw a tall man walking out, wearing a police uniform. I was startled for a quick second, but then Ingrid turned, shook the man's hand, and smiled at him.

The man just nodded and turned to walk toward the front door. As he passed me, I could see his name tag—it read "Sheriff Bradford."

What was the sheriff doing in Ingrid Sanders's office? I thought, but Ingrid started walking toward Sophie and me. We stood, looking up, as Mrs. Sanders was quite tall wearing high-heeled shoes.

"So good to see you, Sophie." Ingrid opened her hands in a welcoming gesture. "And you too, Leo." She smiled at me and gestured for us to follow her to her office.

I looked up and saw Nancy from the corner of my eye, peeking from behind a wall near the top of the staircase. It must have been hard for her to see Sophie in her own house.

Ingrid showed us into her office, which was big and white and had three large windows on the wall to the left that showered the room with bright sunlight. The wall to the right was lined with shelves covered with pictures of Mrs. Sanders with other smiling people who looked important.

Mrs. Sanders walked Sophie to the corner of the room that had an old desk with a big, shiny computer screen on it. The desk was to the left of a much larger table that faced the front of the room and three heavy leather armchairs.

I stopped and stood behind the three chairs.

"I'm so excited to have a website. I hear that every important institution has one these days. More and more people are getting online. It's crazy how fast the Internet is growing. Right?"

"Yes, it is." Sophie nodded.

"So did you make good progress?" Ingrid asked as they got closer to the computer desk.

"It's finished," Sophie replied confidently. She sat down on the chair next to the keyboard. Ingrid rolled a chair from the bigger desk and sat down beside her.

"Good—I see the computer is already connected to a network," Sophie started. "Let me pull up the website." Sophie's fingers started tapping the keyboard rapidly. About a half minute later, the website showed up on the screen. I got closer to be able to see it.

A logo of The Good Shepherd foundation appeared on the top-left corner, and several strips with pictures of smiling people filled the screen. The central part of the page had Ingrid's portrait picture with an "Ingrid Sanders for Mayor" label next to it. The strip below had links to different sections of the website.

Ingrid got closer and leaned over to get a better look at the screen. Sophie walked Ingrid through the menu items and showed her the different pages of the website. She pointed at various sections on every page and explained how people could put their name in a form to support Mrs. Sanders's campaign.

Ingrid was nodding along with Sophie's explanations, and I noticed that she was getting more and more pleased with what she was seeing. When Sophie finished, Ingrid sat up straight in her chair.

They were facing each other. Ingrid was so much taller than Sophie, but to me, it seemed like Sophie was looking at Ingrid at eye level. Ingrid smiled and nodded, looking satisfied. Sophie stood and walked to the other side of the desk.

"This is much more than I expected," Ingrid said. "It's a great piece of work, Sophie. I'm starting to understand why you are attracting so much attention at school."

Ingrid opened a drawer in the big desk and took out a checkbook. She opened it, scribbled quickly, and handed it over to Sophie. Sophie took the check and looked at it.

"This is only two hundred and fifty. It's half of what we agreed upon." Sophie looked up at Ingrid and handed the check back to her.

Ingrid gently covered Sophie's hand with hers, folding the check inside Sophie's palm, and said, "Don't you worry, darling. You will get the other half and...a little bit more." Ingrid stood, walked around the table, and got closer to Sophie. She leaned on the edge of the desk.

"There is an election rally that my foundation is organizing next week, and I would love if you would be my guest of honor. I will pay you more if you do that. What do you say?" Ingrid crossed her arms with a little grin on her face.

I was watching this from the side of the room, my hand resting on one of the three office chairs. A bright ray of light washed Ingrid Sanders's face and her blond hair. I imagined this as a scene from a comic book and envisioned the tall, blond woman and the dark-haired girl standing in front of her as two opposites or two rivals fighting each other.

"How much more?" Sophie inquired.

"Ha ha, a businesswoman." Ingrid chuckled. Suddenly her smile disappeared from her face, and she said, "I will double your pay."

Double her pay? That would be a thousand dollars, and Sophie could have enough money for the immigration lawyer.

Sophie didn't show any sign of excitement. She stood, thinking for a couple of seconds, and then put the check in her pocket. She replied, "OK, I'll be there."

"Wonderful! I'll send you an invitation with Nancy tomorrow. You are invited as well, Leo." Ingrid turned to me with her radiant smile.

Ingrid tilted her head to look at something behind me. I turned and saw Nancy peeking into the room through a crack between the double doors.

"Nancy, dear, come on in. Come see what Sophie built." Ingrid waved her hand, inviting Nancy to stand next to her. Nancy looked uncharacteristically shy and walked slowly toward her mother. She stood in front of Ingrid's chair, between her and the screen. Nancy gazed at the screen with her lips pursed. I was surprised by how differently Nancy behaved in front of her mother from the way she did at school.

"My campaign is now online. It'll help Mommy win the election. Isn't that great?"

Nancy didn't reply and just nodded slightly.

"OK, then. Nancy, would you be so kind to show Sophie and Leo to the front door? I have a couple of things I have to finish here. And thank you again, Sophie, for your impressive work. I'll see you soon." Ingrid turned back to her desk, and we both followed Nancy to the door.

As we were walking out of Ingrid's office, Ingrid suddenly added, "Oh, and one more thing, Sophie."

We all turned and saw Ingrid turning her office chair toward us. "If you don't mind, I would like you to say a couple of things at the event. Don't worry; I will write something down, but it would also be nice if you could say a couple of words about what you want to do when you grow up or something like that. Sounds good?"

"Sure. I can do that." Sophie nodded.

"Great. I'll see you next week." Ingrid smiled and turned her chair to face the computer desk again.

We turned back to Nancy, who was already exiting the room toward the formal living room.

As we walked out through the front door, Nancy leaned on the doorframe.

"I still mean what I wrote in my note—you're going to get what you deserve!" she said, sneering.

Sophie stopped and turned to Nancy. She got close to her until their noses were only a couple of inches apart. "I hope I will," she whispered, and she turned to the open driveway.

I stood close to Nancy as well. I felt angry and gave her the nastiest look I could come up with as I walked out to join Sophie.

"If she doubles your pay, that's the missing one thousand dollars you need!" I said excitedly when I caught up with Sophie.

"Yeah, but I have to get through that election rally first. I wonder what Ingrid is up to, wanting me onstage there."

Then I heard Sophie whisper, "Maybe I shouldn't have taken that offer," and before I could say anything, she started running.

"Hey, Soph, wait up," I shouted, but Sophie just kept running and disappeared behind the trees of the curved driveway.

I knew it would be better not to follow her.

CHAPTER 14

BEWARE OF THE DO-GOODERS

"Leo Weckl, don't you know how critical your eighth-grade grades are? You better sit down and learn!" My mother kept bugging me about studying for final exams, so I spent most my afternoons studying and hardly met with Sophie. Sophie was busy herself—she worked most evenings and spent her free time in front of that computer in the library.

The election rally was fast approaching, and my mother was spending every afternoon helping to organize the big event slated to take place at the fanciest hotel in town.

My mother was excited that Ingrid Sanders had invited me to the rally, although she had mixed feelings about the reason behind my invitation. "This atheist girlfriend of yours—I don't like her," she said to me at dinner.

"She's not my girlfriend, and you don't know a thing about her!" I yelled back before going up to my room for the rest of that evening.

On Thursday evening, the night of the election rally, I dressed up nicely. My mother had bought me a brand-new dark-blue suit and a black tie.

"The whole town is buzzing about this event. You don't know how hard it is to get on the invitation list. People who don't know Ingrid well enough had to pay a lot of money to buy a seat," she said as she tightened my tie around my neck. "Every important person in this town is going to be there, Leo. So you better be on your best behavior, you hear me? The congressman, the governor, Mrs. Sanders, the head of our workers' union—those are influential people, you know?"

"Yes, Mom." I shrugged and tried to loosen the tie a little bit.

The day before, I had asked Sophie about going to the rally together. I was looking forward to going with her, but she'd said she had to take her mother to the doctor and might even run a little late.

My mother and I drove to the rally in our car. She was nervous and excited and told me all the details of how Mrs. Sanders's campaign volunteers had put this event together.

"Ingrid must win this time!" my mother said as we got closer to the hotel.

The hotel entrance was beautiful. Rows of bright lights hung from the ceiling, lighting the hotel entrance. Dozens of flower arrangements rested on white marble stools, and bellboys in black uniforms ran around helping people out of their cars.

"I have to go and help out at the desk. You behave, you hear me?" My mother pointed at me as we approached the revolving doors that led to the main lobby. She left, and I found myself staring at the enormous entrance hall.

Couples dressed in suits and fancy dresses were walking up the hotel lobby staircase. Large The Good Shepherd Charity Foundation and Ingrid Sanders for Mayor signs were posted on stands all the way from the entrance and across the hall to the main ballroom. People were laughing and talking loudly, and reporters scrambled to take pictures and talk to guests, scribbling quickly in their notebooks.

I followed the signs to the main ballroom. To the left of me stood a banner with the same picture of Sophie and Ingrid from the newspaper article. When I got closer to it, I noticed that somehow Mr. Palmer was missing from it. It was just Sophie and Ingrid below a title that said, "Ingrid Sanders will increase the public education budget!"

I walked through the long hall and into the ballroom.

It was enormous, and it made me feel small. The ceiling was extremely high, and the columns on the sides of the hall looked like thin rocket ships waiting to soar into the sky. The light was dim, and the candles on the tables created a mesh of little, flickering flames multiplied by their reflections from the wine glasses.

A hostess walked up to me and asked for my name. She checked the list and smiled when she found it.

"Follow me," she said, holding a card with my name on it. I followed her as she walked straight through the center aisle, which was paved by a dark-red carpet that looked like it was cutting through the tables, straight onto the main stage.

Two spotlights that came from different corners in the back of the hall lit the stage. They crossed each other right at the speaker's podium, which looked like it was elevated a little too high. It reminded me of our church's altar. On the front of it was a big poster of Ingrid Sanders smiling. "Our Next Mayor," it said in big, red letters.

A thin, black microphone was sticking out from the podium, pointing its head up like it was waiting for the evening to begin.

The hostess turned left to the second row of tables and pulled a chair for me. Two people were already sitting at the table—a mother and her six- or seven-year-old son, who fidgeted next to her. The mother looked rather young, but her skin was wrinkly, probably from too much time under the sun.

The woman held her child's hand, and they both looked nervous, almost frightened of what was going on around them.

Suddenly, I saw an envelope lying on our table with the name Sophia Anwar written on it. I grabbed it and laid it in front of me. It was not sealed, and I could see it was a card with text written on it.

Ingrid's speech for Sophie, I thought.

It was 6:55 p.m., and the event was to start at 7:00 sharp. I saw Ingrid Sanders talking to a large group of people next to one of the tables on the other side of the red carpet. More and more people entered the big hall, slowly filling the seats around the tables.

"Where's Sophie?" I heard a stern voice ask from behind me. I turned around and saw Ingrid Sanders with a sinister look on her face. "She is on the speaker list. I need her here!" she continued.

"She's coming, she…she took her mother to a doctor, but she'll be here," I mumbled, quite nervous from Mrs. Sanders's tone of voice.

"She'd better be. And tell her to make sure she reads exactly what is on the card here." Ingrid Sanders pointed at the envelope on the table in front of me, then turned and walked back to the group of people in the front of the room.

At 7:02 a man in a black suit got up onstage and announced that the event would start shortly. I saw no sign of Sophie and was beginning to get worried.

Gradually, the noise of people murmuring died down, and Ingrid Sanders came onstage. Suddenly, everyone stood and started clapping and cheering, looking at Ingrid, who was smiling her big smile, walking, and waving as the two spotlights followed her toward the podium.

I was looking back to the ballroom's entrance, hoping to see Sophie entering, but there was still no sign of her.

"Thank you, thank you, everyone, for taking part in this special evening. You guys know that I am running for mayor, right?" Ingrid paused, and everyone laughed. "But more seriously, if you ask me why I am doing this... once again..." She paused to allow for the murmurs from the audience to quiet down. "I would say that it is not really my choice. I feel it is my duty to serve this community and make sure that each and every individual in it benefits from our collective wealth and prosperity. It is our moral duty to get rid of the awful inequality that Joe Triolesta created in this town. It is time we take care of our poor, our sick, and our unemployed, who long for our compassion and their social justice." Ingrid raised her voice in the last sentence as if cueing the audience to stand up and cheer.

"As mayor, I will make sure that the rich, the privileged, and the, unfortunately, selfish part of our society all pay their fair share." Ingrid raised her voice, and another round of applause filled the big hall.

"I want to start with someone very near and dear to me, my father, our state governor—Bill Sanders." Ingrid smiled and lifted her arm toward the table just below the stage. Once again, the entire room was on its feet, applauding. The mother and son sitting next to me were standing as well, apparently not understanding why.

The governor was an older man; he was bald, and he had a fat belly and a red face. He was limping as he walked up the stairs and stood next to Ingrid. He hugged Ingrid and then stepped up to the podium while waving to the audience.

The room became silent, and just before the governor started talking, I heard people murmuring and whispering behind me. I turned around and saw Sophie standing on the red carpet in the middle of the hall.

The governor noticed something was happening and paused, shading his eyes from the spotlights to look for the reason for the murmuring.

Everyone was staring at the girl standing in the middle of the room.

Sophie was looking around calmly, ignoring the hundreds of eyes that followed her as she walked slowly, scanning the left side of the hall looking for me. I waved, and Sophie immediately spotted my hand and started walking toward our table.

Sophie wore a long, white dress with wide shoulder straps that emphasized her dark skin. She carried a small purse, and her hair was woven into a braid. A thin strand of hair was coming down from the edge of her forehead to her cheek as if it had escaped from its place in the long, loose braid.

Her dress was simple but looked like it was the perfect one for her. The white fabric fell from her shoulders, curving around her waist and floating down to her ankles, moving gently with every step she took. Her face was calm and peaceful, and I watched her as she approached me, feeling like her smile was directed at no one else in that crowded room but me.

I pulled out a chair, and Sophie sat next to me. Then, like it was the obvious thing to do, I extended my hand below the table and took her hand in mine. I held her hand for a couple of nervous seconds.

"Beautiful dress," I complimented Sophie.

"My mother sewed this one as well." She smiled and tightened her grip around my hand. I wondered why I had waited so long to hold Sophie's hand this way and why only now, in this crowded event, I'd found the courage to do it.

The governor, who seemed a little annoyed by the interruption, looked straight out at the audience and started talking as everyone became silent again. His voice was deep and loud, and he kept waving his hands in the air, pausing from time to time, signaling to the audience when they should clap and cheer.

"This is for you." I pushed the envelope on the table toward Sophie. Sophie opened it and read it carefully. She took a pencil out of her purse and started writing on the card.

"It needs some corrections. Our school is not as great as she wants me to describe it." Sophie smiled, her head still lowered toward the card.

I knew it wouldn't help if I told her that Ingrid wanted the card read word for word.

The governor was finishing his speech.

"We are here today to strengthen our commitment to the values that we all hold dear as Americans. Vote for Ingrid Sanders!" The governor raised both his hands upward as the audience cheered loudly for a long minute.

Ingrid went back on stage again and kissed her father on the cheek as he walked off.

"Thank you," she said. "I want to talk a little bit about the problem of inequality. One of the biggest problems of our society today is the inequality and the widening gap between the rich and the poor. In the community that I want to live in, people would be equal. No one is going to be too rich or too poor. We are all going to live in perfect harmony, protecting our Mother Nature and sharing our resources."

"Just like ants," I heard Sophie mutter under her breath. I noticed Sophie was getting uneasy in her chair. She was scanning the people sitting around the room as if to check their responses to what Ingrid Sanders was saying.

"What's wrong? She just wants to be the queen ant," I joked, but Sophie didn't find it funny. Her eyebrows pressed together, and she was frowning.

Ingrid invited the mother and child sitting next to us onto the stage. One spotlight turned to them, and the child, who seemed to be startled by the bright light, grabbed his mother's arm, clinging to her like a frightened kitten.

The mother stood up. One of the hostesses walked up and led them onto the stage. They both stood behind Ingrid. The child was looking up to his mother as if to get clues on what was going on and what he should be doing next.

Ingrid smiled at them and turned to the audience. "It was the middle of a hot summer day. I was standing at a traffic light, and this young lady and her precious child were walking between the cars, begging the drivers for money with an empty can. As I passed by them, my heart ached so bad, thinking about this child wandering with his mother in the streets of our very own city. At that moment, I felt an urge to do something about it. I decided that on top of the programs we are running, we should start a tradition of donating directly to the ones in need. I'm hoping that you'll join me and open your hearts and wallets this evening so that we can donate much more to families in need in our community. It is our duty. *We are* our brothers' keepers."

The crowd gave Ingrid a standing ovation, and she waved back at them.

The child on the stage got even closer to his mother, hugging her leg. The mother stared down at the floor.

"I want to invite my father, our governor, to hand this family a donation check together with me. If it weren't for him, I wouldn't be standing here." Ingrid smiled. One of the hostesses escorted the governor back onto the stage and handed him a big cardboard check. She then led the mother and her son to the front of the stage so the photographers could take their pictures with Ingrid and her father.

The mother suddenly put her hand to her mouth and started crying. As Ingrid handed her the check, she suddenly bent over, bowing in front of Ingrid.

"It's OK; it's OK." Ingrid hurried to the mother to make her stop bowing awkwardly. Ingrid signaled to one of the hostesses to escort the mother and her son down from the stage.

All this time, Sophie was staring at what was happening onstage. Her hand still held the pencil on top of the speech card, her face fixated on the mother and child. Her mouth opened slightly, and she looked as if she was shocked or appalled.

As the mother and son came off stage, I saw a woman at the back of the stage hand a second cardboard check to the governor.

It was for a thousand dollars.

My heart started racing. *That's for Sophie!* I thought as I turned to look at her. It was just as Ingrid had promised; she'd doubled Sophie's pay.

Sophie was frozen. She didn't move and just stared at the stage. Suddenly, she shoved the card into her purse and stood up.

"What are you doing?" I asked in a loud whisper as I pulled my chair closer to her.

"What does it look like I'm doing? I'm leaving!" Sophie answered impatiently.

As Sophie started moving, I grabbed her purse to stop her. "You need that money, Sophie! You can't leave now!" I said quietly but firmly.

Sophie pulled her purse back, but I didn't let go. She pulled it again, and suddenly, its strap tore, sending the purse to the ground with Sophie's card and pencil spilling out of it.

As I leaped out of my chair and knelt to grab the purse up from the carpet, I heard Ingrid announce, "And now for a special guest of mine."

A spotlight moved to focus on Sophie, who was standing, looking down at me collecting her things.

"Sophia Anwar," Mrs. Sanders said, and everyone turned to look at Sophie.

"Sophia is a brilliant young lady from a single-parent family who is showing great potential. She is a product of our wonderful middle school, in which I'm personally involved as the chair of the board. Recently, Sophie scored the highest score in the entire state on the standardized test." Ingrid Sanders paused, and the crowd cheered for several seconds.

"I've visited Sophie and her mother in their home. Let me just say that a girl like Sophie deserves better conditions than the ones she currently has. And this is why we've decided to award Sophie the sum of one thousand dollars to help her fulfill her potential as a contributing member of our society." Again, the room filled with the sound of applause.

"I am sure that one day, our community will get repaid by her future contributions. She is smart; she is tough, and I'm sure you'll understand why we are so excited about this young girl. Please welcome Sophia Anwar to the stage!" Ingrid Sanders gestured at Sophie with a big smile, inviting her to the stage.

The audience was clapping, but Sophie didn't move.

She looked at the stage and then down at me.

I was squatting on the carpet, looking up at her. We stared at each other, and for some reason, the sounds of clapping faded slowly away and became muted as if they were getting farther and farther away from us. For a brief moment, the room disappeared around us. It was just Sophie and me in this big hall, looking at each other. My heart started beating fast again, and I felt a rush of blood flush through my face and then throughout my whole body. I wanted to jump up and hold her, but then, as if things were still happening in slow motion, Sophie's gaze shifted with one slow blink from my hands holding her purse back to Ingrid Sanders on the stage.

A spotlight was aimed right at her from the side of the room, making part of her face shine with bright white light and covering the other with a dark shadow. The audience was still clapping, cheering, and looking at the girl with the big black eyes and the highest test score in the state.

Sophie started walking slowly toward the stage and climbed the three stairs leading up to it. I stood and went back to my chair, anxious about what was to come next.

The governor, who stood beside Ingrid in the middle of the stage, was holding the cardboard check, looking like he planned to hand it over to Sophie, who was walking toward him and Ingrid. But Sophie didn't stop.

She passed him and Ingrid and continued to walk straight to the podium. Ingrid was confused for a second but then put on her big smile again, facing the audience as if this was all part of the plan.

Faint gasps of surprise rose from the audience, but the room became silent as Sophie reached the podium.

I leaned back in my chair, still holding Sophie's purse, trying to figure out what was going through her mind.

Sophie took a moment. She looked around the room, squinting against the spotlights' brightness.

"First of all," Sophie said calmly, looking back at Ingrid, "I want to correct something: I'm *not* a part of a single-parent family. I have a father. He is just not here."

Ingrid nodded with an accepting smile. Sophie turned back to the podium and faced the slim, black microphone again.

"Secondly, I think that I am a product of my grandfather's teaching more than school. I'll explain. When I was eight years old, my grandfather had me memorize the Declaration of Independence. All thirteen hundred and twenty-three words of it. And he spent quite a bit of time explaining why the beginning of the second paragraph, about man's inalienable rights to life, liberty, and the pursuit of happiness, was the seed for the freest, most prosperous society in human history—this place. America."

The room was still totally silent. I looked around, and everyone seemed to be focused on the girl in the white dress, who spoke in a clear, confident voice.

Sophie lowered her head for a brief moment and then continued, "This document and its ideas allowed people to come here from all over the world with nothing and create a life for themselves. Like the one I want to create for *myself.* They were left free to pursue their own happiness—by themselves, and without a government controlling their lives. Without handouts or free checks from politicians who force it away from productive people, just to hand it to others, while keeping a chunk for themselves."

The audience started murmuring loudly; people turned and looked at one another with concerned faces.

Suddenly, Ingrid Sanders started moving toward Sophie, but her father grabbed her firmly by the wrist, stopping her. When she turned to him, he nodded to her and whispered something in her ear, barely moving his lips. Ingrid Sanders turned back to stand next to him, reluctantly. Her face was red and her lips pursed, and I thought I could never have imagined Ingrid looking so enraged as she did.

Sophie turned back for a quick second and looked at Ingrid Sanders. Then slowly she turned her head back to the front of the stage.

I realized I was still holding Sophie's purse in one hand and her speech card in the other. I slowly laid them on the table in front of me.

Sophie started talking again over the fading murmur of the audience. "My happiness is important to me, and I know that I will have to earn it. I cannot get it from anyone else. That is why I only expect to get what I deserve. Giving money to people who didn't earn it just makes them weaker and more dependent—it never makes them happy." Sophie turned to look at the mother and child, who were sitting on the other side of my table.

"My grandfather told me something interesting. He said, 'Be suspicious of strangers who claim to care for you. Trust the ones who deal with you, admitting they do it for their own sake. Beware of the do-gooders!' he said. So Mrs. Sanders..." Sophie turned to the back of the stage. "Thank you for inviting me to this event, but all I want is for you to pay me the other half of the money you owe me for building your website. Thank you."

Before Ingrid could respond, Sophie stepped down the stairs and walked across the room on the red carpet toward the exit. Everyone started chattering loudly as Sophie's long braid disappeared down the hallway.

Confusion and commotion spread across the ballroom. Some people laughed, some looked worried, and some were just looking at one another and the stage. Ingrid Sanders walked up to the podium and started talking. "I'm sorry you had to hear this. I can assure you it was not part of this

evening's plan," she said over the noise of the crowd that was still not set-
tling down from Sophie's speech.

Some reporters ran out to the hall to chase Sophie.

I ran outside as well. I looked down at the lobby from the top of the big
staircase and saw Sophie running out of the hotel's main entrance. She out-
ran the reporters, and they turned back empty-handed toward the main
hall.

CHAPTER 15

MESSING WITH POWER

The following week was one of the most challenging weeks of my life. I was confused and angry; thoughts and emotions swirled in my head and my stomach.

Stories about the girl who had crashed Ingrid Sanders's election rally filled the local newspapers. People were talking about it everywhere.

"It is time someone stood up against the corrupt Sanders 'royal family.' I don't know that girl, but I like her already," Mayor Joe Triolesta said in an article on the front page of one of the newspapers. Other reports said that Ingrid Sanders was dropping quickly in the election polls.

Sophie did not show up to school for the entire week. I passed her house many times and stood next to the oak tree for hours, waiting for her to come out. I saw reporters gathering around her house and some even knocking on her door, but she was nowhere to be found. Later, after they left, I walked up to the door and knocked on it myself, but there was no answer.

Finally, that Friday afternoon, I gathered my courage and walked to the Mediterranean restaurant at the strip mall, near the ice cream place with the plain chocolate flavor I loved.

I walked to the back of the restaurant, as I didn't want anyone to see me. I saw a window into the restaurant's kitchen that was too high for me to see through. I gathered a couple of crates from the nearby trash container and stood on them, leaning on the wall while holding the windowsill with both my hands.

I looked inside and saw a cook standing in front of a high table that had a bowl of potatoes in it. He was peeling the potatoes in swift movements while potato peels flew all over, landing on the floor beneath him. He was peeling them so rapidly that he finished peeling the entire bowl in what seemed to be less than a minute. He sliced them quickly and then turned to the other side of the kitchen, which had a large stove with pots on it. He lit a flame and set a big pan on the burner. As he was starting to pour oil into it, Sophie entered the kitchen. She held a bucket in one hand and a piece of cloth in the other, and she walked toward the table where the cook had just peeled the potatoes.

She started collecting the peels into the bucket with the cloth. The way she was gathering the potato skins with swift, circular movements looked to be almost as efficient as the cook was. They didn't seem to notice me, so I felt comfortable sticking my head a little higher to get a better look at what was going on in the kitchen.

The cook turned to Sophie and said something in Arabic. He was pointing at the floor. Sophie nodded, laid the bucket on the floor, and grabbed a mop that was leaning on the wall behind her. She went around the high table, closer to the cook, and started cleaning the floor around the stove and the cook's feet. She leaned forward, applying pressure with the mop to clean a dirty spot on the floor. A thin strand of her black hair was getting in her face, and the last thing I saw was her hand gently pulling it behind her ear.

A second later I was hanging in the air.

Someone grabbed me from behind, lifting me up by my waist. My feet were dangling over the crates on which I was standing. I was startled and afraid as I felt strong, thick arms squeezing my hips, not allowing me to turn back and see to whom those arms belong.

"What you doing here?" a deep, accented voice asked from behind me.

"I...I was just...just looking for a friend of mine. She...she works here," I stuttered.

"Who is that?" The man was still holding me firmly.

"Sophie," I mumbled.

The man put me down on the pavement and turned me around. He was a tall, large man with a big mustache. He held me firmly by my shoulders. "You mean Sophia?" The man said her name in a way I'd never heard before and then started laughing. I was confused and still afraid this big man was going to hurt me in some awful way.

"You her boyfriend? I don't know Sophia had boyfriend..." He smiled.

"Oh no. Not a boyfriend, just a...just a friend." Under different circumstances, I'm sure I would have blushed, but I was too afraid for that.

He took his hands off my shoulders and said, "OK, you, but next time no come sneaking from back, you hear me?" He pointed his finger at me. Then he opened the restaurant's back door and went in.

"Sophia!" he shouted as he went through the kitchen door.

I was frozen and didn't know what to do. A second later, Sophie opened the back door and walked up to me. Her face was sweaty, and she had a dirty apron around her waist.

"Where have you been?" I asked as she got closer to me.

"Working, mainly," she answered and crossed her arms over her chest, "when I'm not dodging reporters or other people who want to kill me for what I did the other day."

I shook my head feverishly. I was angry with her, and I couldn't hold it in. "Why *did* you do it? I don't get it! It was so stupid to risk everything like that!"

Sophie stared at me with a stern look, her arms crossed over her chest. Then suddenly, she looked away, her face contorting and her lips quivering. Tears started coming from her eyes silently.

She turned back to look at me and said quietly, "I thought that you, of all people, would understand."

"Sophia!" a loud voice suddenly cried from within the kitchen.

"Hey," I said, getting closer to Sophie. "I..." I started to say something and then hesitated for a second or two.

Sophie did not hesitate. "I need to go. Don't tell anyone I'm here, OK?" She turned and walked quickly toward the cook, who stood at the restaurant's back door, holding it open and looking at both of us. Sophie ducked underneath the cook's arm and disappeared back into the kitchen.

I stood there frustrated, thinking of all the things I could have said to Sophie instead of having a brain freeze.

I walked back to my house. As I got closer, coming out of the back trail of the neighborhood's park toward our backyard, suddenly I blurted, "Stupid!"

I couldn't tell if I'd said it about Sophie or myself, but I felt bitter and angry—about Sophie, myself, and about the whole situation.

As I turned from the side of the house to the front, I saw Ingrid Sanders's car in our driveway. I climbed the stairs up to our front porch and suddenly heard my mother and Ingrid Sanders talking. The front door was open behind the screen door. I stood behind the wall to the side of the entrance.

"Triolesta is almost running out of campaign money. He said so in to-day's meeting," my mother said quietly.

"Good. Maybe we can contain the damage by bombarding the media with ads. This way he cannot retaliate, which will show weakness," Ingrid replied. "Thanks for the information, Annie. I have to go; I'm late for another meeting."

I tiptoed quickly around the side of the house so Ingrid would not see me. I heard the screen door open and then saw her get into her car and drive away.

I heard my mother's heels clacking back into the house and the door closing behind her. I waited for a couple of minutes and then went into the house. I stopped in the kitchen to get a glass of water.

My mother was there, organizing the groceries in the pantry. She looked at me as I gulped down the water.

"What?" I asked, wiping my mouth with my sleeve.

"You've seen her, haven't you?" my mother said quietly.

"Who?" I replied.

"You know who, Leo. Don't play games with me. Where did you see her? Tell me." My mother closed the pantry door and stepped closer to me. It'd been a while since I'd seen my mother so upset.

"You mean Sophie? I didn't..." I tried to think about what to say.

"Leo Weckl, you listen to me now." My mother got even closer. "That girl caused so much damage that I can't even start to describe it. Now, do you know where she is?"

I felt rage. It sounded like my mother was determined to hurt Sophie somehow, and that was why she wanted to know Sophie's whereabouts.

"It doesn't matter if I know or not. I wouldn't tell you anyway!" I said.

My mother opened her mouth, shocked by my response.

I put my glass down on the countertop and walked out of the kitchen, through the living room, on my way to the staircase leading up to my room.

"I don't know why I let you spend so much time with this girl. I'm to blame for that!" my mother screamed behind me. I turned to face her and saw her standing on the other side of the living room, nodding. "But it doesn't matter anymore." My mother stood up straight, wiping her hands on the sides of her dress.

"What do you mean?" I took a step forward.

"That girl will not be here for much longer." My mother nodded again and pursed her lips. I couldn't determine if she was happy or sad, but I could see she was getting emotional.

I took two steps forward and stood on the other side of the dining table.

"Yes, Ingrid found out that Sophie and her mother are here illegally." My mother put her hands on her waist.

My heart ached in my chest. I leaned forward on the table with both my hands, trying to digest what my mother was saying. The thought of Sophie being in danger and the thought of my mother being part of it felt like too much to bear.

"Oh, I don't know why you care so much for that girl, Leo. She's no good—can't you see it?" my mother asked, adding insult to injury.

I wanted to scream and shout at her. I wanted to let her know that I knew she was betraying the mayor, but I decided not to say anything I would regret later. I stood, looked at my mother with teary eyes, turned, and rushed out of the house, slamming the door behind me.

I sprinted through the park and out of the neighborhood, my heart pounding but my feet not slowing down. I let them carry me back to the restaurant.

I got closer to the restaurant and ran around it, planning to knock on the back door, but as I turned the corner, I saw Sophie coming out of it.

"Hey, are you OK?" she asked. I leaned forward in front of her, my hands on my knees as I breathed heavily. Sophie put her hand on my back and bent over to look at my face.

"What happened?" she asked. I guess my face was already telling the story.

"It's...it's Ingrid, she knows about you being illegal...she found out about it." I stood up, still breathing heavily.

"Oh." Sophie raised herself up but stayed calm. "That means we don't have much time. Let's go now." She grabbed my hand and started walking.

"Where? Go where?" I asked as I started following Sophie, her hand pulling me forward.

"Look at this," she stopped and shoved her hand into her pocket.

Sophie took out what looked like a roll of money strapped together by a yellow rubber band. She handed it to me.

"What's this?"

"I didn't get paid for two months. I asked Hamid, the restaurant owner, to save it up for me. He just gave this to me. It's seven hundred and fifty dollars, finally enough to pay to start the immigration process. All I have to do is pay the lawyer and submit the papers, but we have to hurry now. The lawyer's office closes at five."

"You're amazing, Soph..." I handed her back the money, and just as I was about to start running, Sophie grabbed my wrist.

She pulled my hand down gently, making me take a little step forward. I was standing close to her, enough to feel her breath. She looked up at me with her black eyes and with the same strand of hair resting on her cheek.

"You're amazing too, Leo," Sophie whispered.

I grabbed Sophie by the sides of her shoulders and pulled her toward me. Our mouths touched, and we kissed the gentlest and softest kiss. I opened my eyes and saw Sophie's eyes closed in front of me. She was smiling with her eyes closed for a couple of seconds before she opened them slowly.

And then we started running.

The lawyer's office was about a mile away on Main Street, near the city hall building. The place looked like a house that had been converted into an office. It was white, had a dark-gray roof, and had a gate with a big black sign with golden letters that read "Gordon & Krugman, Attorneys at Law."

We ran through the gate toward the front of the office. Just before we got to the stairs, leading to the entrance, I slowed. Sophie didn't stop and continued up the short staircase leading to the office door.

I looked to the left side of the house's big, circular driveway. Three cars were parked there, one after another. The last car, which was closest to the building, looked familiar. It had a pearl-white color I recognized.

Before I could turn to Sophie and tell her who that car belonged to, she had knocked on the door and gone into the office.

I ran up the stairs and went inside.

Sophie stood in the middle of a large waiting room in front of the reception desk. A tall man with a dark-gray suit, who seemed to be the lawyer, was standing behind the receptionist. Ingrid Sanders was standing next to him.

The receptionist turned back to look at the lawyer, shocked. The man's face was pale, his eyebrows pushed up, creating furrows on his forehead. He looked concerned, almost scared.

Ingrid was grinning. "Wow." She shook her head slightly. "Right on time, Sophie. I couldn't have planned it better if I'd tried."

Sophie didn't look at Ingrid and was still staring at the tall man.

"What is she doing here?" Sophie asked him.

"I... I...," the man mumbled and turned to look at Ingrid.

"He is the only serious immigration lawyer in town. Didn't you think I'd figure it out?" Ingrid crossed her arms over her chest, with a smug smile on her face. "Interesting how we ended up here at the same time, isn't it?"

Sophie still didn't turn to look at Ingrid. She stepped forward, took the money out of her pocket, and held it up toward the tall man.

"There are seven hundred and fifty dollars here. It's what's left to cover the five thousand you said you needed to complete the application." Sophie paused, and the tall man didn't move or blink. He just stood there, frozen.

"You said that if I gave you five thousand dollars, you'd make sure that we're safe. That the application would go through, and we'd be fine, right?" Sophie took another step forward with her hand still up in the air.

"So here it is—take it." Sophie elevated her hand some more.

The lawyer turned slowly to look at Ingrid Sanders again. Ingrid did not move and just looked at Sophie with a sly grin, her arms crossed over her chest.

The sound of a car driving on gravel came from outside the open door.

"I think it's a little too late for that," Ingrid Sanders said quietly.

Someone was climbing out of the car outside, slamming the door behind them. I heard the sound of heavy steps getting closer to the office, and then a big man came through the door.

It was Sheriff Bradford.

The sheriff took a long look around the room and then took a step forward toward Sophie.

"Sophia Anwar," he said in a low, deep voice, "I will have to detain you for violation of US immigration law."

Sophie took a couple of steps back, and Sheriff Bradford took a quick step forward.

"Please don't move," he said, pointing at her. Sophie's back was against the back wall of the waiting room. To her left was a hall that led to several closed office doors. Sophie's eyes darted among the sheriff, the lawyer, and Ingrid Sanders.

She turned to the lawyer. "But I've started the immigration status change process, Krugman!" she exclaimed, looking straight at him.

"Well..." the lawyer tilted his head apologetically. "Not officially. I didn't file the papers yet. I'm...sorry..."

"We will have to go now, Sophia." Sheriff Bradford took another step forward. "I will drive you back home for you to take some things, OK? And don't worry; your mother is coming with you." The sheriff tried to sound gentle.

Sheriff Bradford put his hands on top of Sophie's shoulders and turned her toward the door. Sophie looked at me and then at Ingrid Sanders.

"A lesson not to mess with people more powerful than you, kid. Enjoy your freedom in Syria." Ingrid Sanders looked both disgusted and satisfied at the same time.

"Don't," the sheriff muttered to Ingrid. He looked disappointed as he exited the room with Sophie.

I felt angry and frustrated. I jumped to catch up with the sheriff and Sophie.

"Where are you taking her? I want to know!" I cried to the sheriff as he walked toward the police car, which had another policeman in it. The sheriff didn't respond and just kept walking, holding Sophie by her shoulders.

"Answer me! Answer me now!" I screamed as the other officer got out of the car and opened the back door for Sophie.

The sheriff finally turned to me and said, "Kid, I'm sorry, but we have to take Sophia and her mother to a detention facility. There is nothing you can do about it. Go home," he said, and got in the car.

I looked at Sophie through the window. Before I could do or say anything, the police car made a loud noise launching itself from the gravel driveway. They drove out of the gate and onto the main road.

A sigh of pain came out of my mouth, draining my chest of all the air in it. I stood there in the gravel driveway, feeling helpless.

The lawyer and Ingrid Sanders came out of the office door behind me. The lawyer escorted Ingrid to her car. Just before she lowered herself into the car, she paused and looked at me.

I stepped forward, and without even thinking about it, I started screaming at her. "Sophie's right; you don't care about anything but power, do you? You don't want to help people—you want to control them!"

Ingrid tilted her head forward. Her eyebrows lowered into an angry look. She wanted to respond, but the lawyer next to her put his hand on her shoulder, trying to calm her. Ingrid pushed the lawyer's hand away from her forcefully.

"You're lucky I know your mother, you little brat," Ingrid hissed. She got into her car and drove away hastily. The lawyer was quick to rush back into his office, looking like he was afraid I would start screaming at him as well.

I turned to look at the open gate Sophie had gone through a minute ago. I felt like the world was not going to be the same from now on. My heart ached, and I was thinking about what to do next.

I started running toward our neighborhood. I crossed several roads right in the middle, signaling cars to slow down with my hands. I ran all the way to Sophie's front gate, opened it, and sprinted up the porch's stairs to the front door. The door was unlocked, and I went in, but it was too late. There was no one in the house.

I dashed to Sophie's room. Her mattress was on the floor, the pile of books stacked next to it, and the bag with the broken telescope sat in the corner of the room. After a moment I saw what seemed to be the corner of a photograph peeking from below the big wall closet.

I bent over and grabbed it. It was a black-and-white photograph of Sophie sitting on an older man's lap. Sophie must have been about five years old at the time, and the man looked exactly how I would have pictured her grandfather—handsome, tanned, gray-haired, and with a groomed beard. He had the same piercing eyes as Sophie.

She must have dropped it when she was packing, I thought and put it in my back pocket. I went out of the house, through the park, and then back to my house.

On my way home, I planned how I would run away and never talk to my mother again, but then I remembered the detention facility. I had to make a plan to get there as soon as possible.

I entered my house. My mother and father were sitting at the dinner table. My mother stood when she saw me come in, but I walked quickly up the stairs and into my room.

My mother came up and tried to talk me into opening the door, but I didn't respond. Luckily, she decided to leave me alone after my father convinced her that I needed some time to myself.

I lay on my bed, my head buried in my pillow. I imagined Sophie in a prison cell behind bars, but somehow, I forced myself up, deciding to focus on getting to that detention facility the sheriff mentioned.

My mother knocked on the door again on her way to bed, trying to get me to talk to her, but I still didn't respond. I had nothing to say to her, and after a couple of minutes, she gave up and went to sleep.

A little later, after I made sure my parents were both fast asleep, I tiptoed down to the kitchen and called 911. I whispered into the phone, asking where they kept people who were about to be deported.

The woman on the other side of the line was kind and helpful.

"The Belleview Family Facility is probably where your friend is. It is about a forty-minute drive south of the city," she said, and she even told me what bus I should take to get there.

I decided to wait for the next morning and catch the first bus there. I made sure I had enough money in my pocket and set my alarm clock for six in the morning.

I kept turning from side to side in my bed for hours that night. I couldn't stop thinking about Sophie locked up in that detention place.

❖　❖　❖

The next morning, I left the house just before six thirty—before anyone was up. I made my way to the bus station and got to the county detention facility about an hour later. It was a foggy morning, and I could barely see the road as I ran from the bus station to the facility's front office.

"Where are your parents?" the officer behind the counter in the front booth replied after I asked if I could see a girl named Sophia Anwar. When I said I was there by myself, he told me he couldn't give me any information because I was not an adult.

"Please," I pleaded. "Sophie is my friend, and she's about to be deported. I have to see her."

The officer just shook his head and said "Sorry, kid—I can't. You have to be accompanied by an adult, and they have to request a visit through an application." He took a piece of paper from his desk and gave it to me.

Frustrated, I took the form and walked back outside. I folded it and put it in my pocket. My hand touched something that was already there, and I remembered I had Sophie's photograph still. I ran back to the booth.

"Officer, can you please give this to Sophie Anwar? Please, sir—it is very important to her."

"I will certainly try," he promised.

It started drizzling. I zipped my coat all the way up to my neck and walked back toward the bus stop, which was just a pole stuck in the ground next to a low wall of old stones serving as a bench.

Maybe I can convince my father to come with me, I thought as I walked on the side of the road.

I heard the sound of an engine behind me. I turned and saw a brown bus coming out of the detention facility. It turned left toward me. I stopped walking and watched the bus as it got closer to me.

It was still going slowly when, suddenly, I saw Sophie's face and hands pressed to the bus window. Her eyes were wide with astonishment, and her hand was holding the picture I just had given the officer a minute ago. It took me a brief moment to realize what was happening, and then I started running next to the bus, which was still slowly accelerating. I could see her clearly for another two or three seconds as the bus kept accelerating away from me. The last thing I saw was Sophie making some type of a rectangular sign with both of her hands and saying something behind the window.

I kept on running and screaming, "Sophie, stop! Stop the bus! Please!" but it just kept going, disappearing into the fog.

I stopped in the middle of the road. I was out of breath and felt a tingling sense of sheer sadness cutting through my chest. The drizzling turned into pouring rain.

I went back to sit on the low stone wall on the side of the road, next to the bus stop pole. I sat down, and without being ready for it, I started crying as I had never cried before.

I took the bus back home.

I walked slowly, dragging my feet as I passed Sophie's house. One of the doors of the tin shed next to the house was open, rocking and swaying in the wind, making a loud squeaking sound. I could see our wheelbarrow with the tools in it. It was standing there, motionless, as if it knew something was over.

I passed by the big oak tree, looking at its leaves swaying in the wind. They rocked back and forth slowly, making a motion that looked like a hand waving goodbye. I turned and walked toward my street.

I recalled Sophie's face in the bus window and tried to make sense of the shape she'd made with her fingers before I lost sight of her.

A post office truck passed me, stopping in front of my house. I saw the mailman opening our mailbox and putting a white rectangular envelope in it.

I knew in an instant it was a letter from Sophie. *That* was the rectangle! She had been trying to tell me she'd sent me a letter.

I rushed to the mailbox and fished the letter out quickly. I immediately recognized Sophie's handwriting, and I opened it, my hands shaking.

I started taking the letter out of the envelope, my heart racing, but decided to go somewhere else. I shoved the letter into the inside pocket of my coat and ran back to the big oak tree. Our tree.

I sat down on the same grass patch where I'd first met Sophie. I took out a white page that was folded perfectly into the envelope. I opened it slowly with trembling hands.

It said:

Leo,

I'm sorry that we didn't get to say goodbye. I wish I could see you one last time.

I wanted to let you know how much I enjoyed the time we spent together. You are the best friend anyone could have, and I will always, always remember you.

I don't know what is going to happen to us, but I'm sure we will manage. So please don't worry about me. I'll be fine.

I hope that you'll continue to be who you are. To draw your thoughts and feelings on paper and create remarkable characters and stories. Follow your passion and don't ever compromise. Even if it makes you suffer in the short term.

I wish I could kiss you one more time. But I can't. Instead, I am sending you an imaginary kiss for all the great times we had together.

I promise I'll write to you as soon as I can. And who knows? Maybe we will meet again someday.

Yours always,
Sophie

A tear trickled down my cheek onto the white paper, but I wasn't crying. I folded the letter carefully back into the envelope, put it in my pocket, and went back home.

CHAPTER 16

THE ELECTIONS

I was lost for the next couple of days. I didn't talk to anyone, especially my mother, and locked myself in my room as soon as I came back from school. At school, the kids were talking and asking about Sophie, but I just said I didn't know where she was. I felt like it was the right thing to do.

Later that night, I went down to the kitchen after my parents went to bed. I was hungry, having missed dinner again that evening. I opened the refrigerator and grabbed a cold piece of pie. I started chewing it and turned around to face the kitchen table. I spotted an open newspaper on the counter.

"Ingrid Sanders leading the polls again!" the front-page headline said. I read the article, which detailed how Ingrid had managed to rebound and lead the election race after the incident at the rally.

The elections were only a week away, and as I swallowed another bite of the pie, I realized what I needed to do.

❖ ❖ ❖

The next day, I skipped school and walked all the way to city hall, where my mother worked. I knew Mayor Triolesta used a back entrance to the building because my mother had mentioned that to my father several times.

I went around the building and waited near the only door that looked like a back entrance. I waited for more than thirty minutes in the little parking lot at the back of the building, rehearsing what I wanted to say to the mayor.

Then a black town car drove into the parking lot. It came to a stop, and the mayor got out from the back door. The driver noticed me and got out of the car as well.

"Mr. Triolesta, sir," I cried as he closed the car door, holding a briefcase. The mayor turned to look at me. He was tall and skinny, and had thick white hair and a pointy nose with frameless glasses resting on the middle of it. They looked like they were going to fall off his nose any second.

The driver, who wore a black suit, turned to look at me and then started moving toward me.

"Mr. Triolesta, I need to tell you something important—please!" I cried again before the man got to me.

"John, it's OK. He's just a kid. Relax," the mayor said to his driver, who turned to look at him. Mr. Triolesta walked toward me with a friendly smile. He and his driver came closer until the mayor stood in front of me, holding the handle of his briefcase with both his hands. He said, "How can I help you, son?"

"I need to tell you something. It's a secret." I looked up at the driver in the black suit. The driver looked at the mayor with a concerned look.

"It will only take a minute, sir; I promise," I added pleadingly.

"OK, now you got me curious." Mr. Triolesta chuckled and nodded to the driver.

We walked several steps together and stood closer to the building's back wall.

"I'm Leo. Leo Weckl. I am a friend of Sophie...Sophia Anwar, the girl who spoke at Ingrid Sanders's rally."

"Go on," said the mayor.

"She got deported last Saturday. Ingrid Sanders took care of it." I tried to sound as formal as I could.

"What do you mean 'took care of it'? This is a matter for the police, not Ingrid Sanders." Mr. Triolesta's words were clear-cut and without any emotion.

"Yes, but Ingrid knows Sheriff Bradford very well. I even saw him at her house. Last Friday, Ingrid called him from the Gordon and Krugman office right when Sophie and I came to pay the lawyer the rest of the money for Sophie's immigration process." I recited the words I had rehearsed over and over.

"That's interesting. So you're saying that Mrs. Sanders interfered with Sophia's immigration process?" The mayor narrowed his eyes and gave me a grave look.

"Yes, she did." I nodded confidently.

"Hmm..." The mayor raised his hand to his chin. "This intersects with other information I have on that matter. Thank you for this, son. I will surely look into it." He bowed his head slightly and walked straight into the building through the back door.

The next Monday after I met Mayor Triolesta, our town buzzed as it never had before. The newspapers reported a police investigation against Ingrid Sanders and Sheriff Bradford; it even involved the state governor. "Police are investigating suspicions of bribe and corruption," said the article my father read to me after I asked him about it.

A couple of days later, Ingrid Sanders withdrew her nomination from the race for mayor, and Sheriff Bradford resigned from his position. Investigators found evidence of bribery and mismanagement of public funds, which Ingrid had filtered into her foundation illegally.

Mr. Triolesta won the election, and I watched everything as if it were happening in a movie and not in real life.

CHAPTER 17

ICE CREAM

The red light turned to green. I was live on national TV during prime time.

"Leo Weckl, it's a pleasure to have you on our show finally," the famous young TV host said joyfully, sitting in a chair on the other side of the studio table. Two large cameras circled us, and I felt the warmth of the bright lights directed right at me.

"You've built the fastest-growing video-game company in the world, and its hit game Secrets of Celestia shows no signs of slowing down. I understand it's based on a comic book from your childhood, is that right?"

"Yes," I nodded.

"And you're only thirty-one years old! I want to start by asking you, what is your source of motivation? What drives you?" The host leaned forward onto the table between us.

I sat back in my chair. The program coordinator had sent a list of questions to my office a week before the interview, but I'd decided not to read them. I wanted to be spontaneous.

"Telling stories. I've always liked good stories. I love characters who take you on a journey and the roller coaster of emotions that comes with the constant pursuit—which is what life is all about," I replied.

"What made you leave your position as the chief game designer at Eclektic and start Ophies Games, your own gaming company? It was a bold move right at the peak of your success at Eclektic." The interviewer sounded genuinely interested.

"I had a friend a long time ago who taught me about honesty and integrity. She told me once that honesty is being true to the world and how it works, and integrity is being true to yourself and how you work. At Eclektic, I felt like I could not express my true vision for the heroes I wanted to create. So for the sake of my own integrity, I felt it was time to start my own thing. That friend is someone I consult with, in my head, when I need to make hard decisions, and she was in favor." I smiled.

"She? You're not married, right?" the interviewer asked, tilting his head.

"Ha! No, not yet." I shook mine.

"So who is that person? Where is she now? That's kind of a unique type of influence..." The interviewer leaned forward, and I started to understand why his show was so popular. His questions were straightforward and penetrating.

"Hmm..." I thought for a quick second. I had not been ready for that question.

"I don't know. She left when I was thirteen, and...I never heard from her again. But she is still close to me even though she's not around anymore, and I talk to her in my head from time to time. It's weird, I know, but I do."

"Interesting," the interviewer said, and he went on to ask me more questions about the success of Ophies Games.

The show was a success, and ratings were high.

The next day I got the e-mail.

It looked like a spam e-mail from an unrecognized sender. But right before I hit the delete button, I stopped. The first name made me stop. It said Orthea. The last name was Rawan.

It took me three seconds, and then I swung back hard in my chair, making it roll away from my office desk. I had to push myself forward with awkward little flings of my feet, trying to get the chair back to the computer.

"She took Orthea's name!" I gasped and started reading the e-mail slowly.

My dear Leo. When your face came on TV last night, I nearly choked on my dry room-service sandwich. Your face, your words, and your smile instantly threw me back in time.

You never answered my letters from Syria, and I still don't know if they ever made it to you. All those years I was wondering if you were angry with me or just lost track of me.

I was moved when you said you were still talking to me...

I am on a business trip in the United States next week.

Meet next to our oak tree?

Yours, always,
Sophie

I searched the Internet for anything I could find on Orthea Rawan.

"Orthea is the most brilliant mind in the medical-devices industry today," one article reported; another mentioned that she was the young founder of "Atlas", a revolutionary respiratory technology company, and that her fortune was estimated to be over a $100 million.

I immediately recognized the "Atlas" logo— it was the same one that was on the respirator I bought my mother a year back. It was the best and most expensive one I could find.

❖　❖　❖

And here I am again.

The tree is still here, but the patch of grass is gone. Everything looks older and smaller than I remembered.

It is now a quarter past four in the afternoon.

We were supposed to meet fifteen minutes ago, but there is still no sign of her.

As I turn to look at the rusting playground behind me, a white car turns into the neighborhood. It rolls slowly closer to me and stops.

Sophie smiles at me from the window.

She gets out of the car, walks over, and stands in front of me with a joyful smile on her face. Her jet-black eyes haven't changed one bit, and her look is piercing and focused as always.

"Care for some ice cream, Leo?"